To A',

Caitlyn Fournier ♡

Red Rain

By: Caitlyn Fournier
Cover and Art by: amini101

First Paperback Edition, June 2018

Printed in the United States of American

Other books written by this author:

Stand Alone Novels:

Hated

Hell's Heat

Mutant Series:

Forgotten Magic

Story and Poem Collections:

Difficulty

Magical Collection

Thank you to my family and friends for always supporting my rash and not always smart decisions.

Thank you to my amazing cover artist, amini101, who had both designed the cover and the little sneak peek scene near the end of the book.

To my old manager who had helped me out with connecting the ideas and hearing out my sometimes very odd suggestions that I had, especially when the ideas came while I was working! Thanks Matt!

Chapter 1

It seems to rain every night here.

Beau sat in the small wooden chair that looked out his second story bedroom window, leaning on the well used desk that was directly in front of him. His fingers tracing circles in the rough, chipped paint on the desk top as he lazily watched the water splatter on the window and slowly slide down the glass, seeing it as a race in his own mind as to which droplet would make it to the bottom of the window first.

Beau watched the puddles of water that formed on the dark sidewalk outside the front of the house, and the rivers of water that flowed down the edges of the street, seemingly endless. The street lights were just starting to flick on, one by one. The sun had set only a few minutes ago, but the sky was so cloudy that only long shadows could be seen either around the street lights or in quick bursts whenever there was a lightning strike.

The room that Beau was sitting in was warm and dry compared to what it looked like on the outside, even if the room was a bit on the cramped side. Besides the desk there were two bunk beds and a small tan in colour wooden dresser in the room that Beau shared with three other boys. He could hear some of the other boys that lived in the house playing a game in the next room over, which was one of the two living rooms that were in this three-story house. Beau had thought about playing with some of the other boys earlier, but they just seemed to ignore him or push him away whenever he had tried to join.

This crowded house was the only place that Beau had known to call home. He never knew his parents or if they were even alive, the lady, Ms. Kay, who takes care of everyone here had told him that she had found him in a cardboard box next to a dumpster when he was just a baby. She had skipped over some of the gorier details back then but had told him that that was the reason why he had the scar going through his left eye. Whatever had happened back than was also why he couldn't really see out of that eye either. It made him the target of ridicule both at the house and at the grade school that he went to during the week.

Beau sighed and continued to watch the rain pour down and watch everything be washed away and cleansed in the rain. The rain turned everything it touched into a clean slate. He wanted to go out and run around in the rain and splash in the puddles, and play with some of the other kids, but none of them had the same fascination for the rain that Beau had. Though it was cold and wet, he thought that it was beautiful, fascinating, and magical.

Beau's head shot towards the door of the bedroom when he heard a loud crash that sounded like it had come from just down the hall. He got up from his chair and quickly walked across the creaky, old wooden floor and over to the door to see what was going on out in the hallway. Beau peeked his head out into the hall and saw that a couple of the other boys were dressed in capes with fake fangs, that didn't really fit in their mouths properly.

Beau just shook his head and turned back around to go back into the room when he was caught by the collar of his shirt and was dragged backwards out into the hallway. Beau let out a little squeak in surprise as he stumbled backwards, coughing as the front of his shirt pulled uncomfortably tight around his neck. When the person had let go of Beau's shirt, he was finally able to turn around and see who had decided to roughly drag him back out into the hallway. Beau swallowed hard but stood his ground knowing what was going to come next would only be worse if he showed fear.

"Well hello there, Ghosty," said Kyle, one of the older kids that was sent to the home after his parents were arrested. What they were arrested for, he wouldn't say, and no one had ever really wanted to ask him about it considering how touchy he could get whenever his parents were brought up in conversation. He was three years older than Beau and at least a foot and a half if not two feet taller than him. He had dark brown hair that was kept military short all the time, and his eyes were a chestnut brown that always seemed to burn with an angry fire. He liked to pick on Beau because of what he looked like, since Beau was born an albino and had a large nasty looking scar going through and around left his eye. "What are you doing out of your room?"

"I just wanted to see what all of the commotion was about," Beau replied calmly as he felt his heart start to beat faster. Kyle was about a foot taller than Beau and about three years older than he was. Beau had overheard Ms. Kay talking to Kyle's social worker in the kitchen a few days after he had been brought to her house. It had sounded like his father and mother had been arrested for something to do with drugs and battery, or something like that, again touchy subject so no clear details. Either way Beau wasn't sure what either of those words meant when he had overheard them, he just knew that Kyle was very mean to him because of it. "I was headed back in when you had grabbed me."

"No, you weren't, I know what you were thinking," Kyle sneered as he poked Beau hard in the chest with a thick finger. *Ow*. "You know that we don't want anything to do with a weird ghost looking scar faced kid like you, so don't even think about coming out of there again just to 'see what's going on' or I will knock you right back in there myself."

Kyle gave Beau a shove backwards so that he stumbled backwards into the room and landed on his butt on the hardwood floor, with Kyle slamming the door directly behind him. He heard Ms. Kay, who was the lady that had taken Beau in, yell from downstairs for Kyle to stop slamming the

doors, with Kyle replying with a meek sorry.
Kyle and other boys were always a lot nicer
to the lady that took care of us, but she was
nice to everyone that came and went from
this place. She did have a bit of a soft spot
for Beau though since she had found him
when he was an infant.

Beau got up from the floor and
rubbed at the sore spot on his butt before
walking over to the bottom bunk of the bed
that was on the left that he had claimed as
his. He had been put into foster care and
almost adopted a couple of times, but each
time fell through. Now that Beau was 12,
fewer and fewer people were coming around
to look at him. He was starting to feel
hopeless that he would ever get adopted and
find a family that he could belong to, but
there was always this small hope in the back
of his mind that his real parents would find
him one day or that someone would want
him.

Beau laid back on the old bed and
stared up at the top bunk as he listened to
sound of the rain and tried not to think about
the sounds of the other boys playing
together just down the hall. Kyle's words did
sting as Beau lay in the bedroom by himself,
all the other boys thought that he looked
weird and even a bit scary because of his

skin tone, scars, and the odd colour of his eyes. Beau wasn't sure which was worse though, the ridicule that he got at his house or the ridicule that he would be getting at school the next day and had been getting since he had started school.

Beau reached underneath his pillow and pulled out a colourful hacky sack, and he began to toss it up in air as he let his mind wander to anywhere else but where he was. He thought about how ridiculous the other boys were being for play acting as vampires. Those creatures were fake and just a bunch of scary stories to keep the other kids to behave, they could never really exist, could they?

Beau caught the sac and held it for a moment as the thought crossed his mind, and for a moment he had the very distinct feeling that he was being watched. Beau sat up on the bed and looked around the room suspiciously but shrugged to himself and laid back down when he didn't see or hear anything out of the ordinary. Resuming throwing the hackie sac into the air and then catching it again as he day dreamed about how life would've been like if he had a family.

Chapter 2

"Come on boys! Or you will be late getting to school!" Ms. Kay yelled up the stairs as all the other boys rushed around on the upper floor, trying to get ready for school. Beau headed down the cramped and steep flight of stairs first as the other boys fiddled and rushed around to get their stuff. Beau had gotten up earlier then the other boys so that he could avoid all the commotion and rough housing that came about in the mornings before school.

Beau reached the bottom of the stairs where he met Ms. Kay, whose name Beau sometimes couldn't remember but he would just call her mom whenever he was talking to her if he happened to forget. She was a very nice lady with wrinkles around the corners of her eyes, and a bit of grey hair starting to come up from the roots of her dark, chestnut brown hair. She turned to look at Beau and smiled when she saw him before turning her attention back to whatever she was working on that was in a big silver pot on the stove.

"Have a good day, Beau, and try your best," Ms. Kay said as Beau came up and hugged her from the side. She hugged him back with her free arm and gave him a quick kiss on the top of the head. The fact that she gave Beau a bit more affection than the other boys might also be some of the reason as to why he was so often bullied by the other boys in the house, but that never seemed to occur to Beau.

"Thanks mom," Beau replied smiling before he ran towards the front door of the house as he could hear the other kids start to rush down the stairs like a stamped of wild animals. He grabbed his black and blue backpack that was hanging on a hook next to the door just before he ran out the front door, closing it behind him as he left.

Outside it smelled like the freshness after a spring shower but the skies were still an eerie grey, and the clouds hung low in the sky, threatening with more rain. Beau walked along the sidewalk, sidestepping puddles, as he made his way to the grade school that was a few blocks from the boys' home that he lived in. He loved the smell that came right after it rained and loved the smell and the look of the dew on the grass in the morning.

Beau really did enjoy school, but he dreaded the other people that were there. He did get along with some of the people there, but there were a few other people there that have been physical with him on more than one occasion. Beau did his best to avoid them, but they always seemed to be able to find him no matter where he went in the school.

Once Beau got to the school he managed to be able to say "hi" to a few of the people that he got along with before the bell rang for the classes to start. Things seemed to be going well for Beau for most of the morning, and even after the lunch break nothing had really happened. This made Beau feel comfortable and unassuming as he went about his day, focusing on his classes for a change.

That was until school had ended, then his calmness and good mood was shattered. Beau was just saying goodbye to some of his friends and was heading around the back of the school so that he could head back home to the boys' home when he spotted a group of three older boys standing in way of the path that Beau usually took to get home. He thought about turning around and taking the long way home since that would probably be the safer alternative than getting into it with those boys. But just as he was about to change direction he could see that the other boys had already spotted him and were now stalking towards him. Beau groaned as he knew that there was no chance of escaping from them and figured that he would have more energy to defend himself if he didn't try to make a run for it.

Beau looked through them and continued walking forward hoping that they would let him pass but knowing in his heart that they probably wouldn't. He was not in the mood to be beaten up today, or any day for that matter. Why couldn't he have just a nice relaxing day where he didn't have to fear being picked on the moment that he managed to be alone for a bit.

"Hey, look at what we have here, if it isn't the snow witch, where do you think your going?" the tallest of the three boys asked as he sneered down at Beau. Beau kept wondering what was with all the ghost and witch jokes, did he really look so much like a person that wasn't human? After having such a good day Beau was a bit more irritated than usual at being stopped by these weirdos on his way home, so he was feeling particularly sassy when he responded.

"To your mother's house, where do you think I'm going?" Beau snapped as he looked the boy directly in the eyes. Watching as what he had said slowly clicked together in the other boy's mind. The look that the boy was giving him made Beau realize that he had just stepped on a very big landmine. The tallest boy gestured to the other two boys and they both grabbed Beau by the upper parts of his arms and pinned him up against the brick outer wall of the school. The last thing that Beau remembered before blacking out was seeing the boy's fist coming at his face, the next thing that he knew he was waking up on the pavement with the three boys already far away from him, laughing to each other as they turned down a side street that lead away from the school.

Beau dizzily got to his feet, his head was spinning, and his vision was going in and out of his one good eye. He gingerly touched around his left eye, which was tender and already started swelling with a cut just above his left eyebrow. Beau touched around his sore jaw and felt blood coming out of the corner of his mouth and from a split in his lip. He thought that he probably really did look like a scary ghost or witch now. He stumbled down the walkway and back towards the boys' home, the only place that he had ever really called home.

Ms. Kay was not going to be very happy to see him coming home in this state again after coming home nearly completely bruise free for over a week, well at least that's what she thought anyway. Beau knew that they had just hit him in places that weren't directly noticeable. Especially after being confronted by both Ms. Kay and the principal of the school the last time that Beau had told them what was going on.

Beau had missed the bus and was forced to walk the rest of the way home with a sore stomach from where they had repeatedly punched him and a pounding headache from where the back of his head had probably kept hitting the brick wall.

Chapter 3

Beau was right about what he thought would happen when he got home. Ms. Kay was very upset about seeing the bruises and the cuts on that were starting to appear on the sides of Beau's face. But seemed a bit preoccupied with a couple of the other boys who had gotten into trouble to really say much else about the incident. Beau was not really in the mood to say anything more about being beaten up anyway, so he took that opportunity to quickly make his escape.

Beau quickly went up the stairs to work on some schoolwork to try to get it done before Ms. Kay called them all downstairs for dinner. Beau sat in his room at the desk that looked out the window and worked away at his homework, completely alone. One of the other boys that did sleep in the same room as Beau came into the room after Beau had been working on his homework for only a few minutes. He said a quiet hello to Beau before grabbing what he had came into the room for and then left the room without another word. Beau sighed as the boy left and resumed his work on his homework, until he could hear Ms. Kay calling for them to come down for dinner.

Beau was at the very least a bit happy that Kyle had seen his bruises and left him alone for the time being. Kyle almost seemed a bit sympathetic towards Beau whenever he saw the bruises that he had received from school. Kyle had never been overly physical with Beau like the boys at school had always been, just verbally abusive with occasional shoving to get Beau to do what he had wanted him to do.

Beau got up from the desk and made his way out of the room and down the stairs to join Ms. Kay and the other boys at the 10-person dinner table that was set up in the dining room. Besides Beau there was eight other boys in the house that Ms. Kay was looking after, the eldest being 16 and the youngest being four years old.

Dinner was always messy with nine boys trying to get something to eat all at the same time, but Ms. Kay set it up as a buffet style in the kitchen so that there wasn't as much stuff to clean up on the table. Dinner was the only time where things were calm and quiet in the house, when compared to the rest of the day. After dinner was finished all the boys helped with cleaning up the table, putting the leftovers away, and cleaning the dishes that had been used during dinner.

"Hey mom, can I go to the convenience store to get some snacks after I'm done with my homework?" Beau asked Ms. Kay after he had finished drying the remaining utensils and had put them away in the proper spots in the drawer. He wanted to get some fresh air in the hopes that Ms. Kay or anybody else wouldn't try to ask anymore questions about anything that had happened today.

"Of course, but try not to stay out too late, it's supposed to rain again tonight," Ms. Kay replied as she didn't look up from the dishes that she was finishing washing in the sink. She then handed them to Kyle to dry and put away in one of the upper cupboards.

"Thank you, mom!" Beau said as he hugged her around the waist before taking off back up the stairs to finish his homework. He didn't have too much work left to do, so it wouldn't take him too long to finish the few pages that he had left. Beau even had a bit of spare time to read the newest chapter in his currently favourite horror novel, *Dracula*. Sure, he didn't believe what was written in the book could ever actually happen, but he liked the idea of someone else being odd besides himself.

After Beau had finished the chapter, he grabbed his saved money that he had earned from running errands and newspaper routes and threw on a dark blue hooded sweatshirt over his white wifebeater shirt. He thought for a moment about whether he should change out of his khaki shorts but decided against it.

Beau quickly ran down the stairs to avoid the prospect of running into Kyle, even though he was being nice now Beau didn't want to take any chances at pushing his luck with Kyle. He said a quick goodbye to Ms. Kay on his way out the door and began his walk down to the convenience store which was only a couple blocks away. It had gotten dark enough outside that the street lights had started to come on as Beau made his way down the street, so Beau picked up his pace a bit, not wanting to be out too late. Even though it was a beautiful night out with the cool breeze that lightly ruffled Beau's hair, he knew that he would get in trouble if he was out for too long, no matter how nice it was out.

The streets and parks were empty of people and the only sounds that could be heard was the occasional dog bark or an occasional car zooming past Beau at a much faster than normal speed. To say that he wasn't at least a bit nervous to be out at night walking around by himself would be a lie. But he felt safer once he had made it inside the convenience store, surrounded by the bright artificial lights and shelves of over priced snacks. Beau looked around the isles and grabbed a couple of candy bars before going up to the counter to pay for them.

As Beau was paying he looked out the glass doors and noticed that it had started raining heavily into the streets. Some of the large droplets splattered against the glass doors of the store making the glass look like it was made of frosted glass. The lady at the countered handed Beau back his change and a receipt before turning her attention back to her cellphone which she had placed next to the computer when Beau had approached the counter.

Beau pulled up the hood of his hoodie and stuffed his snacks into his front pouch pocket of his hoodie as he approached the water splattered glass doors. He walked out of the store and stood underneath the very small awning that was next to the front door as he watched the rain pour down, only inches of awning separating Beau from being drenched. It was a little heavier than he had thought that it would be and was sure that he would be soaked before he had even managed to get halfway back to the house. He took a deep breath in before he took off out from the awning, jogging and hoping that he wouldn't be hit too hard by the rain, but within minutes he was soaked from the heavy down pour. Beau paused for a moment to catch his breath at the entrance of one of the parks that he had passed by on the way to the store.

It was quiet outside except for the sound of the rain that made tinkling noises whenever it hit metal or 'splat' whenever it hit the ground or pavement of the sidewalk that Beau was standing on. As Beau started to catch his breath and regain his senses, he could hear an odd squeaking sound coming from the direction of the playground that was in the middle of the park. Curious, Beau glanced around and squinted into the park in the direction of the playground which was just beyond the light of the streetlamps.

Beau could vaguely see something moving back and forth in the dark near the swing set.

Beau stepped away from the light of the lamppost and towards the squeaking of what must've been the swings, it sounded almost rhythmic. He stopped a couple steps into the park and let his good eye adjust to the darkness, the street lights casting some light into the park from his back. He could see a figure swinging back and forth on one of the swings. It looked like a kid around Beau's age and height, just swinging in the pouring rain. As Beau's sight adjusted further, he could see that the boy was wearing dark pants, that could've been jeans, but Beau wasn't sure, and a dark leather looking jacket.

The boy on the swing tipped his head back like he was looking up at the sky for a moment before he quickly planted his feet on the ground, stopping his movement so fast that Beau took a nervous step back. The speed at which the boy had stopped was inhumanly fast. The boy slowly turned his head to look in Beau's direction, eyes glowing a bright red in the thick curtain of darkness. Beau stumbled backwards a couple of steps until he was back on the sidewalk, taking his eyes off the boy for a moment.

23

Beau looked back into the playground after regaining his footing and saw that the eyes and the boy were now much closer. The boy had gotten off the swing and within less than 10 feet of where the edge of the light from the street lamp stopped all in a matter of seconds, but his face was still hidden in shadows. Beau's heart was racing as he watched the other boy watch him, not sure what he should do or if he should even try to run. The boy cocked his head to the side as if regarding Beau curiously, seemingly confused.

Cold water splashed over Beau in a big wave that he half jumped forward and was half knocked forward on to his knees, as it had caught him completely off guard. Beau sputtered and coughed as he tried to dry off his face with his bare hands even though they were just as wet, forgetting that the other boy was still there for a moment. Cursing quietly to himself as he heard the car rev its engine and take off down the road.

When Beau finally remembered that there was a potential danger in front of him, he whipped his head around to look for the boy.

But Beau was now standing in the rain, on the sidewalk, cold, wet, and completely alone.

Chapter 4

"I swear I really did see him mom!" Beau explained as Ms. Kay dried off his head with a bath towel. He had run the entire way home after what had happened at the park, not wanting to take any risks that the kid might still be there watching him form somewhere in the shadows. He had burst through the door soaking wet, dripping water all over the floor of the kitchen in his haste to try to explain what had happened to him to Ms. Kay. Ms. Kay had rushed to get him dried off, chiding him for getting the floor all wet.

"Hold still, you don't want to catch a cold now, do you?" the lady of the house commented as she dried off his hair and face with a smaller towel, and got him to take his sweater off so that she could throw it into the dryer. Beau's shirt wasn't all that wet, but his pants were soaked all the way through from when he had fallen onto the pavement when the car had spooked him. "Now go change your pants and throw these ones into the laundry so that I can get them washed right away."

Beau nodded his head and ran up the stairs to his bedroom after grabbing his candy bars that Ms. Kay had put on the counter next to her after she had taken Beau's hoodie from him. He could tell that his bedroom was empty when he could hear the boys down the hall playing video games, and the younger ones were playing with toys in the room on the other end of the hall.

Beau peeled off his soaked shorts and pulled on a pair of blue plaid pajama bottoms, so that he was in something that was a bit more comfy and warmer. He walked off to the laundry room and threw the shorts straight into the washer before retreating to the bedroom. He was a little disappointed that Ms. Kay hadn't listened to what he was trying to tell her, she didn't believe him at all.

Beau grabbed his copy of *Dracula* off the desk where he had left it before he had gone out to the convenience store, going over to the bed and collapsing onto his back on the bed. Beau held the book up above his head so that he could read while he was on his back though he knew in a few moments he would probably switch to reading on his side, because his arms would quickly get sore from being held in that position above his head.

As he was reading the book something seemed to click together in the back of Beau's mind, something that seemed so impossible but could explain everything that he had experienced earlier perfectly. Beau put the book down on his chest as the weight of what he had just connected settled into his mind and body. Beau realized that when the boy had turned his head up to the sky, in what Beau had thought was to admire the cloudy sky was not actually that, and instead was the fact that the boy had been sniffing at the air.

Beau quickly felt around on his face and felt the raw and open wound that was still splitting his lips from the fight that he had gotten into earlier that day. He thought for a moment that maybe the boy wasn't exactly a *boy* per se. Beau closed the book and flipped it around so that he could look at the cover of the book, the bright red colour was staring back at Beau from the cover. *The boy's eyes were red.* That was the biggest thing that kept popping up back into

Beau's mind that still haunted him and were burned into his brain like he was branded by those eyes.

Beau knew what he saw in that playground; there was absolutely no way that he could've made up something like that. He had been frozen to the spot with raw fear. Beau knew that he could not let that happen again, especially if the boy was as dangerous as Beau presumed him to be. If he were to meet that boy again, he would need to be prepared for whatever could happen and not freeze up like he had this time. Beau planned out that he would go to the library tomorrow and do a bit of research on what he could've possibly seen out there in the park, hoping that his assumptions were wrong.

Beau opened the book again and began to read more before he started to get that funny feeling that he was being watched again. This time though it wasn't so much an absent kind of feeling that he could brush off, it felt like someone was staring at him intently. Beau put his book down beside him on the bed and sat up slowly as he looked around the room for something that could be resulting in the weird sensation that he was feeling, even though he knew that he was completely alone in the bedroom. He knew that he was not going to be able to get any sleep until at least one of the other boys had gone to bed as well, feeling safety in numbers.

Beau thought about going to join the games room with the older boys, and just sit quietly and read his book until they had had enough, or until Ms. Kay had told them to go to bed. But he was afraid about being forcibly shoved out, or worse having one of his only remaining books destroyed by them. Beau sighed in frustration as he wished for a moment that there were any kind of computer or Wi-Fi in the house, however, Ms. Kay didn't want any of that stuff in the house. The only kind of electronics that they did have in the house was a couple TVs and two different gaming consoles that were hooked up to one of the TVs.

Beau laid back down on his bed and got himself underneath the warm blankets. He turned onto his side so that he was facing the wall and picked the book up again, reading a couple chapters until he had managed to drift off into a discomforting sleep with the book held close to his body.

Chapter 5

Beau went to the school the next day with the haunting feeling of the boy's eyes staring at him from the park the night before, and a lack of sleep clouding his mind as he walked along the sidewalk towards the school. Beau yawned and stretched as he walked onto the school grounds but wincing as he stretched his bruised cheek as he yawned. It had already gone on to start turning a dark purple and a bruise had started to form on his abdomen from where he had been punched the day before. Beau's movements were stiff, and his muscles were sore, making him appear to walk with a limp.

No one at the school said anything to Beau as he walked in, even the teachers were turning away like they didn't see what was really going on. Beau knew what they thought of him, had overheard conversations about himself from the students and the teachers. They thought that he was just some troubled kid who would get into fights because he was angry at the world, even though Beau was quite the opposite.

Beau sighed and took a seat in his classroom at a desk that was in the middle row on the far-left side of the classroom, next to the window. His sight issues had caused people to throw stuff at him in class, aiming for his left side where his vision was just that of blurs and shadows. To prevent this, Beau had taken the precaution of limiting who and what was in his blind spot. At one point some of the other students had started a rumour that Beau had cause the scars around his eye himself, since the cuts and burns were too direct to have been from a fight. Even some of the other teachers had started to believe that rumour for a bit before Ms. Kay had jumped in and put a stop to it, explaining the entire situation.

Beau had a hard time focusing in his classes that morning as his mind kept drifting back to the strange boy that he had seen in the park. There was something seriously off about that boy, and it intrigued Beau since he was also very different. He needed to find out more about the boy and decided to go through with his plan to go to the school library after he had finished eating his lunch. He figured that he could check out some books and any kind of websites that he could manage to come up with that may be of any kind of help.

Beau tried his best to focus back on his classes with that now settled in his mind. *If there weren't any problems*, Beau thought, *then it should be easy to get what he wanted to do done.*

When the first set of classes had finally ended, Beau felt like he hadn't really learned anything in those first few hours. His mind had been everywhere else except for being on where it should've been, no matter how hard he had tried to focus. Beau made a quick breakaway towards his backpack and pulled out the money that he had brought with him to buy some of the special lunches that they only ever had on Fridays at the school. Today the special meal from the cafeteria was a cheese and spinach lasagna, that was one of Beau's favourite meals.

Beau made his way down the hallway towards the cafeteria where all the other kids ate their lunches so that the teachers had a chance to set up again for the next set of classes. Beau had nearly forgotten that today was Friday in all the chaos that had taken place yesterday. Now though he was smiling and super excited as he gripped the little bit of earned money, that he had brought with him, tightly in his fist. Beau had nearly made it to the cafeteria when he saw a couple large looming shadow coming up from behind him. He immediately knew that he was in for some trouble, and he wasn't close enough to the cafeteria to book it and hope that he would make it in one piece. But Beau wasn't about to let them just take what they wanted from him, so he did the one thing that he knew that he shouldn't have done, he ran.

Beau had gotten within 12 feet of the cafeteria when he was tackled to the ground. The halls were completely empty, offering Beau no other chance for escaping the three bullies that had just pinned him to the tiled flooring. The two smaller boys had Beau pinned to the floor while the biggest of the three boys stepped on the hand that Beau held his money in. Beau made pained noises as the taller boy stepped on his hand and rubbed it into the ground, until Beau released the money from his hand. He gasped and panted in relief as the tallest boy got off his hand and reached down to pick up the money. The other two boys got up off Beau and followed behind the tallest one as they each high-fived each other and laughed all the way to the cafeteria.

Beau sighed and shook his head as he slowly got to his feet, cradling his injured hand against his body as he wandered off towards the school library to get some research done since he wasn't going to be having lunch anymore.

As he got into the library he immediately went over to the computers and started searching the internet for anything that could have red eyes like the ones that he had seen. As Beau scanned over the sites he could see that there were a lot of things relating to vampires and demons and weird creatures like that. The only thing that looked relatively human and kind of like the boy that he had seen in the park out of all the results that he got was the vampire.

Beau furrowed his eyebrows and looked up different websites that were more specific around the idea that the kid could have possibly been a vampire. But there was this little part of Beau that kept thinking that it was just not possible, that vampires just didn't exist outside of books. However, the way that that boy had reacted to Beau and the abnormal look in his eyes was *not* human.

Beau turned off the computer and just sat in the chair for a moment, staring at the blank screen. He had to have been seeing things that night, it was raining after all, and Beau's face had been a bit swollen since he had been beaten up earlier that day. That had to be it, he had just been seeing things. But the rapid beating of Beau's heart gave away how he really felt about the idea that the boy could've been a real-life vampire.

Chapter 6

After nearly a week of never seeing that weird looking boy again. Beau started to think that maybe he really had just imagined seeing him in the rain that night in the park. He had gone back to the park a couple other nights thinking that if the boy really was a vampire that he would only be out at night, but never had any results. Beau had eventually given up after the third night of no results and just focused back on his school and his newspaper delivery job that he had every Sunday and Wednesday morning. He had been okay during the last two days without too many problems from the boys at school, and Kyle had laid off him for a bit with only the occasional shove in the hallway as they passed each other. Things seemed to be turning around for Beau.

Beau was sitting up in his room with a new book in his hands, this one was called

Interview with the Vampire. It was a bit different from his usual kinds of horror and supernatural books that he normally read. Beau felt like he wanted to try something a bit different in the same supernatural genre. So far it wasn't too bad, but he was thinking that he may have to switch to something a bit scarier than this for his next book though. He pulled his feet up onto the desk and sat back in the rolling chair so that he was in a more relaxed position as he read the third chapter of the book.

Beau's mind wandered to the very odd idea of what it would be like to be friends with a vampire. He put the book down on his chest and stared out the rain splattered window, deep in thought. Having a vampire friend would be kind of dangerous, especially if his friend were to get hungry. Beau rubbed at the side of his neck as continued to think about this and daydream about having a vampire friend. He looked back down at the front cover of the book as his mind slowly switched to the idea of a vampire girlfriend, he laughed to himself thinking that that was completely nonsense.

Beau thought that it could be cool though to have a friend that was a vampire but visiting would be difficult cause Ms.

Kay would probably not approve of his new nocturnal friend. Sleeping patterns would make it difficult too because Beau would have to nap before sneaking out to visit, if he really did want to go. He smiled to himself as he imagined the fun that they could have and the adventures that they could get up to in the night.

His daydreaming was interrupted by a heavy knocking at the door to his bedroom. Beau dropped his feet to the ground and placed the book on the desk as he swung around in the rolling chair to face whoever had knocked at the door.

"Come in," Beau called out and watched as the door slowly swung open, revealing Kyle on the other side of the door. Beau held his breath as he watched Kyle step into the room and quietly push the door closed behind him. There were several beats of silence between the two of them before Kyle spoke up.

"So, a couple of us were looking at going out to a late-night horror movie tonight at the theater, and we were wondering if you wanted to come along too?" Kyle asked as he rubbed at the back of his neck nervously. Beau just stared at him for a second not sure how to respond to his request. He wasn't sure if Kyle was just baiting him or if he actually meant it. "Look I know that you like horror films and books, and I just figured that I'd ask if you wanted to come too, that's all."

Kyle had gestured to the book that was sitting next to Beau on the desk. Beau glanced back to the book and then back at Kyle. He really did want to go because he hadn't seen a new horror movie in ages, since he usually watched the older films because they had a better story and less excessive amounts of gore compared to the newer films. So, he was very tempted to say yes to Kyle's offer of a movie night. Kyle appeared to be getting impatient as his face started to get red like it does when he starts to get angry. Beau nodded to Kyle before verbalising his response as well.

"Sure, it sounds like fun, what time would we be going?" Beau asked as he looked Kyle straight into the eyes. That seemed to make Kyle a bit uncomfortable since he looked away from Beau's eyes, this reaction had always confused Beau no matter how many times it happened.

"We were thinking about trying to get the 10 o'clock show so that it should let out about midnight or so," Kyle replied as he stared at a spot just above Beau's head. Beau was practically oblivious to how uncomfortable Kyle was really feeling since he was a bit too young to completely understand.

"Cool, I think that I have enough money left for it and some snacks if you guys want to share a popcorn or something," Beau replied as he stared at the ceiling, thinking about whether he had enough money to be able to get a big enough popcorn considering that he had had some of his money stolen by some school bullies earlier that week.

"Alright, cool, I'll come back and get you when we are going to leave, which might be a bit early so that we can hopefully get some good seats," Kyle replied as he turned around and grabbed the door handle, pulling open the door. Kyle turned his head around so that he was looking back at Beau. He opened his mouth to say something but seemed to think better of it because he closed his mouth and left the room, closing the door softly behind him.

Beau, though a bit weirded out, was happy at finally being invited out to a movie by a few of the older boys. It had been ages since the last time he had gone out because

Ms. Kay didn't like to go and see horror movies or thriller movies. Beau picked the book back up again and began to read the next couple chapters as he waited for Kyle to come back in and get him for the movie.

Beau had gotten about halfway through the book when he heard another knock on the door. Beau looked away from his book and towards the door as he heard it open. His head was hanging backwards off the bed as he laid on his back with the book in his hands. He had gotten uncomfortable after sitting in the old rolling chair for nearly an hour.

"Come in!" Beau called as he pulled himself up into a sitting position and turned around to face the door, placing the book on his pillow as he crossed his legs sitting in the middle of the bed.

"Hey, we are going to start walking down to the theater, are you ready to go?" Kyle asked as he peeked his head around the bedroom door towards where Beau was sitting on the bed.

"Yep!" Beau replied as he hopped off the bed, his money rattling around in his pocket as he had grabbed it earlier so that he wouldn't forget to bring it with him.

"Alright, let's go, and don't slow us down, got that?" Kyle stated as he narrowed his eyes at Beau in a threatening manner. Beau nodded quickly and nearly jogged out the bedroom door, ducking underneath Kyle's arm which was leaning against the doorframe of Beau's room. Beau made his way down the stairs, spotting two other older boys standing by the front door, with Kyle following close behind him.

Chapter 7

After the movie was over it was nearly 12 o'clock at night when Kyle, Beau, and the two other boys that had come with them exited out the side of the movie theater. They had had an argument at the theater about which movie they should go see, since there were a few thriller and horror movies that were playing that night. The other boys and Kyle had wound up asking Beau to pick the movie since none of them could decide. Beau picked the one horror movie that none of the boys had suggested but Beau had seen some very good reviews about it being super scary. The other boys had meekly agreed not thinking that the movie was going to be really all that scary since the poster was a bit unassuming.

Kyle and the other two boys were chattering away as they walked out into the streets on the way back to the boys' home, trying not to show how scared they had really been by the movie. But Beau snickered from where he walked a couple steps behind them. He knew better than to believe all this bravado that they were displaying since he had seen and heard first hand how scared they really were of that movie, he knew better than to say anything about it though.

As the boys had started talking smack to each other, the other two that Kyle had invited started scraping with each other on the sidewalk. Kyle who was the eldest of all of them sighed and tried to break up their fighting. Beau took a few steps back so that he wouldn't get pulled into the fight, that put Beau directly in front of a dark alleyway that cut between two different apartment buildings, underneath a bright street lamp.

The hair on the back of Beau's neck stood straight up as he stood in front of that alleyway. At first Beau had thought that it was just excess nerves that usually came after he watched a good horror movie. But it distinctly felt like Beau was being watched from within the alley. He rubbed the back of his neck and ignored it for a moment hoping that he was just being over attentive to his surroundings. But the feeling wouldn't stop and got more intense the more that Beau tried to ignore it.

Beau slowly turned his head to investigate the alley and saw the boy that he had seen in the park in the pouring rain, crouched on all fours on top of the industrial sized garbage bin that was about halfway into the alley. He was staring back at Beau with those same haunting, glowing red eyes. The light from the street lamp was just strong enough that Beau was able to see the actual physical features of the boy more clearly.

The boy had some sort of red substance smeared around his mouth and splattered on his hands, Beau thought that it kind of looked like blood and tried not to look at the red stains too closely. The only other reason that Beau was able to see the boy so clearly was that the boy was only about 20 feet away from where Beau stood, much closer than he had been the last time that they had met. Beau was frozen to the spot as he stared back at the other boy.

The boy cocked his head to the side like an animal before jumping down off the dumpster and landing on the ground on his two feet. He was wearing the same jacket and pants that Beau had last seen him in, but the shirt that he was wearing underneath the jacket was a royal blue colour and on his feet were a pair of black combat boots. The other boy stood and stared at Beau for a moment, a bit of curiosity sparked in his red eyes and his face had relaxed with just having one eyebrow raised.

Every part of Beau's body was telling him to run as his heart pounded loud in his chest, resounding in his ears, but his curiosity made him take a couple steps closer to the alley. He wanted to know for sure as to whether or not he was seeing things or if the boy was really standing there in front of him. The other boy narrowed his eyes and took a couple aggressive steps towards Beau, an odd primal growling noise was emanating from the direction of the other boy. Beau figured that his ears must've been playing tricks on him and he scrunched up his eyebrows in confusion.

Even with the blood on his face and hands the other boy didn't really look all that different from any other boy that he knew from school, *maybe the blood was from the boy having hurt himself?* Beau knew deep down though that that was highly unlikely considering that the blood looked dried, and the boy seemed to be walking closer to him without too much of a problem. Beau steeled himself and walked to just beyond the edge of the alleyway entrance. The other boy stopped about four feet away from Beau, making Beau more able to see him in the clear light of the street lamp.

The two of them really were the same height, but while Beau had white hair, because of his albinism, the other boy had black hair that looked almost black-blue in the light of the street lamp. His hair was buzzed at the sides but there were at least a couple inches long of hair on top. Both of their skins were beyond pale, the other boy's skin was on the verge of being light blue with the dark blue strings that were running through his skin around where the larger veins would've been. The dark blue strings snaked around the parts of the boy's body that Beau could see and onto parts of the boy's face.

"What...what are you?" Beau asked quietly, his voice a bit shaky since he was still more than a bit unnerved by the odd-looking boy that was standing dangerous close to him. Beau never took his eyes off the boy, fearing that if he looked away either the boy would disappear or that it could wind up being dangerous for Beau. He knew for sure now that the boy was not in any way human. "Who are you?"

The other boy opened his mouth presumably to say something, Beau immediately noticed his fangs that stuck out a bit further than the rest of his teeth. He was surprised to see that the other boy had double sets of fangs on the top and bottom, rather than the usual single pair on the top and bottom that he had presumed that all vampires had. The boy stopped and stared just behind Beau, his ears twitching slightly at the sides of his head. Beau assumed that he must've been listening to something that he couldn't hear. The boy narrowed his eyes as he hissed and growled low in his throat, glaring at the one side of the alley. Beau turned his head to look and saw that Kyle had come up right next to the alley way.

"Hey, come on, or Ms. Kay will be mad that we got home so late," Kyle said as he turned back around and headed off with the other boys, waiting a couple feet away for Beau to follow them. Beau turned around quickly to look back into the alley but saw that it was completely empty. A sense of disappointment filled Beau, before he hesitantly ran off to join the other boys, not noticing the shadow that was watching him from the rooftop of the apartment building.

Chapter 8

Beau was now sure that he wasn't making things up or seeing things when he saw that same boy in the alleyway after they had left the movie theater. He had briefly mentioned it to the other boys and Kyle as they walked back to the boys' home. The two boys just kind of laughed it off but Kyle gave Beau this weird look that he couldn't decipher and didn't say anything other than hurrying us the rest of the way home. Beau now knew that the boy was a vampire at the very least, which was why he never really got the chance to ever see the boy again after the incident at the park. No one else seemed to believe him whenever he mentioned what he had seen in both the park and the alleyway but that didn't deter Beau, not this time.

Beau had told Ms. Kay about seeing the boy both times that it happened, but she had just brushed it off as him telling stories and making stuff up. Kyle would change the subject whenever he was around Beau when Beau had brought up the topic of the other boy. It was almost like Kyle was either very afraid of the subject or just wanted to avoid it and act like it never happened. Beau thought for a moment that Kyle might know something more than what he was saying but he never got the chance to ask him since Kyle started to avoid him after that night.

Going back to school on the Monday didn't really help Beau out that much either as he couldn't really talk to anyone about what he had seen, mostly because no one would listen, and no one really paid him any mind. Beau found it so frustrating that he wound up spending the next couple days of school lunches in the library doing research on vampires, what were their strengths and what could be their weaknesses that Beau would need to know about in order to protect himself. One of the days while Beau was at the library he had decided to try to see if there were any missing children reports or any early deaths of 12-year-old boys that looked like the one that he had seen.

There were a lot of reports of missing kids around that age but none of them really looked like the boy that Beau had seen. Then Beau started to get into the old history records, photos, and old newspaper clippings thinking that the boy was probably older than he looked. He didn't really find any photos that helped but there was an article that peaked his interest with the headline of "The Last Heir Dies Young". Beau pulled up the article and scanned through it looking for important or relevant information. It was about the only remaining heir to a very rich family who was a 12-year-old boy who was dying from the disease that had apparently killed off the rest of his family over the last few years, but the names were blurred out in the article. That was the only thing that had really piqued his interest from the research that he had done in the library.

Beau prepared questions in his head for when he met the boy again but as the days started to pass by, the boy seemed to have disappeared again. The bullies at the school had taken this lapse in Beau's attention and focus to take advantage of him. They were able to more easily sneak up on him and knock him around a bit before taking off. Ms. Kay didn't even notice that he was getting knocked around more because they aimed for his legs and his midsection, and other areas that were more covered up and less likely to be noticed by prying eyes.

Beau had tried to stay more focused after he had wound up with a big bruise on his chest, but they always seemed to catch him when he was at his weakest. The frustration was starting to build up in Beau and he spent more and more time alone in his room or just going out to get some fresh air for long periods of time, sometimes without permission. Some nights Beau would even stay up late reading his books so that he would be able to sleep without really dreaming about anything. He just didn't understand why no one believed him about nearly anything that he was trying to explain, and that part made him the most frustrated.

Beau was now into a new book after having gone through three other books in his frustrated state, this one was called *Pet Cemetery*. He was laying on his bed with the window on the far side of the room opened a bit to allow the fresh spring air to come into the room. He was flipping through the pages not really paying attention to what he was reading, his eyelids getting heavy. He dropped his book onto his chest, thinking that he could sleep in tomorrow morning because it was the weekend. He felt like he had closed his eyes for only a few minutes when he heard a knocking sound. Beau groaned and rolled over trying to go back to sleep, but the knocking became a bit louder and more urgent.

"Come in," Beau said groggily as he sat up in bed and looked towards the door, only to hear the window open the rest of the way. Beau woke up rather quickly when he heard something drop to the ground in his room with a loud crash after it had rolled off the desk that was by the window. Beau just stared at the thing on the floor, panic clawing at his throat. Smoke rose from the thing that was laying on the floor as the wind blew the curtains around, revealing that it was dawn as Beau could see the sun rising in the distance.

Beau shakily got up from the bed and hesitantly inched over to the dark mass on the floor. He poked at it with his foot and heard a pained groan come from it. As the sun shone in through the curtains, it hit the thing on the ground causing more smoke to rise off it and an awful smell, the thing made more pained noises as it lay there in the rising sunshine. Beau shimmied around it and went over to close the window and shut the curtains, before turning back around to stare at it from the back. Beau was completely surprised that the other boys hadn't woken up with all the noises that the thing had made when it had fallen in through the window and off the desk.

Now that the room was dark Beau had to fumble around on his desk for the flashlight that he kept somewhere in the top drawer. Beau winced when he accidently poked his finger with a safety pin that was in the drawer before grabbing the flashlight. He flicked it on and pointed it at the thing that was on the floor as it began to stir and try to inch towards Beau, making quiet gurgling noises. Beau quickly got his finger to stop bleeding by sticking it in his mouth and cleaning off his finger, the thing on the floor stopped moving.

As Beau looked at the thing on the floor, he could see clothes, fingers, limbs, and some hair on the top area of what must've been the head of what Beau guessed was a person lying on his bedroom floor. The hair looked vaguely familiar with its black-blue colour and what must've been the body was covered in a black leather jacket and black jeans. Beau realized slowly, since he was still partially asleep, that he was looking at the person's back who was laying on his left side. He shimmied around to the front of the body and shone the light back down on the body.

Beau gagged when he saw the festering blisters on the boy's face, and the burnt and blackened skin on his hands and neck. The smell of burnt flesh and singed hair filled the room, making the other boys groan and roll over in their beds. Beau vaguely recognized, underneath all the burnt flesh and blisters, that it was that very same boy that he had met both in the alley and in the park. Beau panicked for a second as the boy's dark, practically black, blood dripped from his wounds and onto the wooden floor of the bedroom.

Beau knew that the other boys were going to be getting up soon and seeing some random wounded kid splayed out on the floor would not bode too well for Beau, not that anyone would really believe him if he tried to explain it anyways. He figured that the only thing that he could really do was to hide the vampire somewhere and maybe patch him up a bit if he could remember what Ms. Kay had used to do for him whenever he had gotten really hurt, besides having taken him to the hospital. But for the life of him, Beau couldn't remember anything that Ms. Kay had done besides wiping the blood off his wounds with the occasional addition of a bandage. This was a lot more blood than Beau had ever seen before and he was starting to kind of feel lightheaded at the sight of it all.

What was he supposed to do with a wounded vampire laying in the middle of the floor of his bedroom?

Chapter 9

Beau ran down the hallway to the bathroom where he grabbed one of the older washing rags, wet it with some water, and, praying that no one had woken up yet, ran swiftly back to the bedroom trying not to make a lot of noise. He had no idea what he had planned to do yet, but if there was a mess left on the floor than the other people that were in the room would start asking questions and pointing fingers, so he had to at the very least clean up the boy and the mess that he had made on the floor. Beau slowly opened the door to the bedroom to keep it from making any noise as he entered, closing it just as carefully behind him.

Beau froze when he walked into the room, noticing that the boy had moved from the position that he had left him in. The vampire boy was now much closer to the storage closest that was on the left side of the room, positioned at the foot of the bottom bunk which was Beau's bed. Beau hesitantly walked closer to the boy and tried his best to steely himself so that he didn't appear as afraid as he really was. The boy was making quiet but painful sounding wheezing noises from where he lay, at least Beau knew that he wasn't like dead dead yet, just regular vampire dead. As Beau got closer he could hear what sounded like some light snoring coming from the body and Beau allowed his shoulders to relax forward as he realized that the boy was most likely asleep.

The boy didn't even flinch when Beau approached him and knelt behind his back. Beau had a sharp intake of breath as he saw that the boy's wounds had already started to heal up, but there was still a lot of blood on the boy's body and on the floor that needed to be taken care of. Beau kept thinking that this was so not like the vampire books that he had read only a few weeks prior. Beau scrubbed at the blood that was on the floor first, which came off the wooden planks surprisingly quickly.

Beau stopped, hovering over the boy with the cloth in his hand, wary about whether he should clean him off as well while he was at it. Beau just shrugged to himself and gently whipped the blood off the boy's hands, then his face, and then his neck, revealing discoloured splotches of skin with dried blood rimming around the edges of the discolouration. Beau made a disgusted face as he saw the extent of the burn marks, with some of the skin flaking off and curling up around the edges of the burns. There was no way that Beau was going to touch that, but now he had to figure out what to do with him so that no one else would find him.

Being directly in front of the storage closet Beau just figured that it was a better hiding place than nothing. He walked over to the desk and rifled around in the drawers looking for the key that would unlock the closet. Beau groaned when he grabbed hold of at least a handful of different keys. He shuffled over to the door and started going through the keys and trying them in the lock that was on the door handle.

Beau was practically through all the keys when finally, using the second to last key, Beau was able to finally unlock the closet door. He put the other keys back into the drawer before walking back over to the closet. Beau pulled it open as far as it would go before puzzling over the body of the other boy. *How was he going to get him into the closet?*

Beau hooked his arms underneath the other boy's armpits and pulled as hard as he could, slowly dragging the boy's body backwards and into the closet. Once the boy's body was in the closet Beau fell backwards onto his butt with the amount of strain that it took to get the body that far. Beau winced and tried to rub the pain away from his backside before getting up from the floor. Beau wasn't too sure what else he could do to hide him, so he walked out of the closet, closing the door behind him, and locking it up tight.

Beau thought about putting the key back into the drawer that was in the desk, and had even gone over and opened the drawer, but paused with the key in his hand over the drawer. He didn't want anyone else to accidently go into the closet and find the vampire boy just laying in there on the floor. Beau's mind wandered back to Dracula and the people that had found him and hunted him down. It made Beau wonder that if vampires really did exist, then would that mean that vampire hunters would also still exist? He didn't want anyone to find him, especially not a hunter.

Beau riffled through the desk drawers again, looking for...*something*...he wasn't too sure what yet though.

"Yes!" Beau exclaimed quietly to himself as he victoriously held in his fingers a long piece of string. He looped the string into the hole that was in the top of the key and tied the string around his neck. Beau was happy that the string was long enough to hide the key underneath the shirt so that no one else would know that he had it on him. He knew that Ms. Kay would be very mad at him if she found out that he had taken one of the house keys. Beau locked the closet door back up, before putting the key on a string around his neck like a necklace and went back over to sit on his bed.

Beau held the key in his fingers and twirled it around as he stared at, the sun beginning to peek in through the curtains as it rose higher in the sky reflecting slightly off the silver key as it reached where Beau was sitting. Beau smiled to himself before tucking the key back into his shirt, hiding it from view. The cool metal bounced lightly against his chest before it settled just to the right of his heart.

Chapter 10

When the other boys had woken up, Beau was still sitting on his bed but with his newest book open in his hands, the silver key hidden underneath his shirt. He had gotten up from the bed shortly before this to change into some day clothes, which was what he was wearing as the other boys crawled out of their beds having slept surprisingly deep the night before. Beau was still surprised that they had slept in as late as they did, considering what had taken place just a couple hours ago. Beau could vaguely hear the other boys moving around in the other rooms as the rest of the house slowly started to wake up. A couple of the other boys gave Beau a funny look as they saw that he was already dressed and reading that early in the morning.

Once Beau had made sure that the other boys had left the room, he let out a heavy sigh. He was very relieved that none of the other boys had noticed that anything was out of place, and that none had bothered to try to get into the closet. But the anxiety came back when Beau realized that he wouldn't be allowed to open the closet for the entire day, and if anyone tried to find the key for the closet, things could get very annoying especially if Ms. Kay had a spare key for the closet.

Beau got up from the bed and went downstairs to help with breakfast, if it wasn't already ready yet. He wanted to tell someone about the vampire kid in the closet, but after the last couple times that no one believed him, Beau wasn't too sure if he really could say anything to anyone. Now that he was thinking about it, it would be even worse if they did believe him. Beau wasn't sure that it would be a good idea anyway because, what would other people do to the vampire kid? Beau squashed the idea of sharing his knowledge with anyone, especially not anyone in the house.

"Hey, do you want to grab the plates and utensils from the cupboard?" Ms. Kay asked as she saw Beau come down the stairs and enter the kitchen. Beau nodded and went about setting up the table for breakfast before it became too chaotic with all the other hungry boys coming down the stairs. "Are you excited for the weekend?"

"Yes mom, I'm hoping to finish my book before Monday," Beau replied as he set up the cups at each of the table spots. He could hear Ms. Kay sigh loudly behind him, but he chose to ignore it and continue to set up the table.

"Don't you think that you should try to go and hang out with other kids around your age?" Ms. Kay said as she brought some of the food over to the table. Beau immediately thought about the vampire boy in the closet who looked about his age and thought that maybe he could at the very least hint at him.

"I think that I might, but we'll see if he even wants to hang out," Beau mentioned as his mind was running with different thoughts about the boy upstairs, *do vampire's even play like normal boys do*, he wondered as he finished setting the drinks down onto the centre of the table. Just as he walked back over to the kitchen to bring the food, Beau could hear the stampeding of feet coming down the stairs towards them. Beau quickly took a seat as he waited patiently for things to calm down before he could grab his own food.

As Beau munched quietly on his breakfast, pushing the chaotic sounds that were coming from around the breakfast table into the back of his mind, he worried about going to school and if Ms. Kay would try to get into the storage closet in his room. Beau tried to soothe his mind with the thought that he was fairly certain that he had the only key to that closet. Besides he had never actually seen someone try to enter that closet for as far back as he could remember.

After Beau had finished eating and helped to clean up the table from breakfast. Once he was done with that he grabbed his school bag and headed for the door so that he wouldn't be late to walk to the school. Once Beau got to the school, his nerves only heightened, as he stared at the buses that drove past him to the school as they dropped more kids off and drove away. *No going back now, he just had to try to relax*, Beau kept telling himself as he walked into the front doors of the school as the bell rang for the classes to start.

Chapter 11

During the last half of the last class of the day, Beau was at the point where he was starting to get impatient and began to tap his pencil on the desk. He had had trouble focusing on all his classes that day, but they were all easy to be able to get caught up on later. Beau had to restrain himself from bolting out the door of the classroom and out to the bus stop when he finally heard the bell ring for school to end. Each step that Beau forced himself to take at a regular pace was just making Beau jumpier, especially as he stood at the front of the school waiting for the bus to take him back to the boys' home.

Most of the time he would just walk to or from the house but on days like this where Beau just couldn't think clearly, he opted to take the bus so that he didn't have to focus on his surroundings as much.

Beau couldn't relax, even as he sat on the bus on the way home. He started thinking up excuses in case someone had managed to get into the closet just to be safe, but it was difficult to come up with an excuse that Beau would be able to think himself was believable enough to use. He gave up and hoped that no one had gone into the closet as the bus approached his stop. Beau got off and made his way down the street to the boys' home, dreading every step that he took. Beau was on edge as he entered the house, and its uncommonly quiet demeanor. He quickly made his way up the stairs towards the hallway that lead to his room.

"Beau!" he heard Ms. Kay call him from somewhere on the lower level. Beau paused on the stairs and took a few steps down so that he was standing in the middle of the stair case.

"Yes?" Beau called back as he peered around to try to find out where the voice was coming from. She appeared from around the corner of her sitting room and glanced up the stairs at Beau.

"Do you happen to know where I put the key to closet in your room?" Ms. Kay asked as she smiled sheepishly up at Beau. "I seem to have lost it again."

The small key suddenly felt heavy around Beau's neck and he swallowed hard as he tried to put on his best not-guilty face, before coming up with a response.

"No, but I'll let you know if I find it," Beau replied before whipping around and practically running all the way up the stairs and into his room. He absolutely hated lying to her, especially after all that he knew that she had done for him, but it wasn't like she would believe him anyway.

He had to wait until after everyone had gone to sleep before he could even think about wanting to open that closet again. He had to try to keep himself busy until then and try not to act any different than he normally did. So, he just holed himself up in his room, pretending to read while chancing glances at the locked closet. The eerie quiet disturbed him more than it usually did.

Beau was relieved when he was finally called down stairs for dinner. Kyle stared at Beau for a moment as he sat down at the table, joining the rest of the boys, with a weird look on his face. Beau scrunched up his eyebrows at Kyle before turning back to eat his dinner, doing his best to ignore the weird look that Kyle kept giving him from across the table. Beau made a mental note to avoid Kyle if he tried to ask him anything after dinner and in the following couple days afterwards.

After dinner Beau was right about needing to avoid Kyle, because right after dinner Kyle had tried to approach Beau and ask him if something was wrong. Beau just answered that he was fine before continuing up the stairs and going back into his room, not coming out again until it was time for bed.

As Beau laid in his bed staring up at the bunk that was above him, waiting for everyone else to fall asleep, he tried to act his best like he too was also asleep. But he could hear a light rattling and thumping coming from the closet and prayed that no one else in the room could hear it. Beau's hands began to shake as he held the blanket up around his neck and waited to hear the quiet snores of his other bunkmates.

Beau pulled the key up from around his neck and slowly slunk out from his bed when he finally heard the last one start to snore. He quickly and quietly walked over to the locked closet door with the key in his hand. Beau's hands shook as he approached the door hearing a scratching sound coming from the other side. It took him several attempts before Beau to be able to unlock the closet door because of how badly his hands were shaking. He slowly turned the knob and pulled the door open, peeking around the crack in the door, but there was nothing there.

Beau pushed open the door the rest of the way, dumbfounded. *Where the heck had that vampire boy gone off to? He hadn't broken out of the door and there weren't any windows in the room or anything else that he could've used to escape out of it.*

Beau saw a dark shadow come at him from one of the upper shelves and it tackled him onto the wooden floor with a loud thud. Beau stared up at the boy, having never been this close to him before he was able to see some things more clearly even if all the light that he had was from the full moon that was slinking in through the curtains from outside. The boy had a tight grip on Beau's upper arms and snarled down at Beau.

Beau was not really thinking about being in any kind of danger from the vampire that was on top of him for the moment, but rather how loud and disruptive the vampire boy was being. Beau had managed to quickly pull out of the boy's grip after lunging his head forward enough to surprise him so that he would be able to cover the other boy's mouth with his hands. He glanced around, afraid that the noise may have woken up the other boys that were still sleeping in the room.

The vampire boy stared down at Beau, confused for a moment as he watched Beau glance around the room. He was wary as to what was in the room that could've been scarier than he was. Beau relaxed and released the breath that he had been holding in his nervous haste. The vampire boy backed away from Beau but stayed crouched at a close enough distance, wary of the human boy. The vampire bared his teeth preparing to snarl again, but Beau put his hands up frantically trying to indicate that he needed to be quiet.

The vampire boy cocked his head to the side and glanced at the three other boys that were sleeping soundly in their bunks. The vampire boy just settled for a low growl instead of another snarl. Beau just nodded and smiled, not sure why he wasn't terrified of the vampire that was crouched only a couple feet away from him which was closer than he had ever been before. Beau was more curious than he was scared and wanted to maybe try to talk to him to learn more about him. Beau sat up and crossed his legs before sticking an arm out towards the vampire boy. The boy bared his teeth and shuffled back.

"My name is Beau, what's yours?" Beau asked quietly being very forward with his approach, almost like he was throwing caution to the wind.

"Why should I tell you?" the boy snarled quietly as he sat up a little straighter. "You had forcibly locked me up in that closet all day!"

"You crashed in through my bedroom window at dawn and I had to try to make sure that no one else found out about you," Beau retorted as he narrowed his eyes, not liking that he was being accused when he had just been trying to help. "Why did you even come here anyway if you thought that I was just going to keep you locked up?"

Beau saw the blue lines become more prominent in the other boy's face and thought for a moment that that was his kind of blushing, before it faded back into being eerily pale. He locked eyes with Beau before his face softened a bit, and he rubbed the back of his head as he looked around the room.

"I-I don't know, I was just trying to find a place that was safe from the rising sun," the vampire boy replied only offering up half of the real reason why he chose to come to this place. Even Beau could tell from the way that the boy was acting that that wasn't everything.

"Did something happen?"

"What makes you think that?"

"I noticed a couple holes in the sleeve of your leather jacket when you tackled me."

The vampire boy looked down at his arms and noticed that his right sleeve had a gaping 3-inch hole going down the upper part of his arm, stopping just above the elbow. The boy pulled off his jacket and even Beau could see the newly formed scar that climbed up the boy's arm from where he was sitting. Beau could also see a circular almost star shaped scar on the boy's upper left shoulder. It took him another moment or two to realize that the sleeve from that arm was missing as well.

"What's that from?" Beau asked as he curiously nudged closer to the vampire boy. The boy eyed him warily as Beau got closer and waited for Beau to stop moving before he responded.

"Last night," the boy responded solemnly, before baring his teeth in a dark smile as he stared off behind Beau, his eyes unfocused. "We had gotten a bit too comfortable while we were out and didn't notice that we were being followed. We didn't see who or what it was even after it attacked us, my family and I were lucky to get out of there. I just don't know if my entire family managed to make it back home before sunrise, they are probably really worried."

Beau stared at the scar in astonishment, thinking that the boy healed inhumanly fast if the wound had already formed a scar in just under 24 hours. But Beau had no idea what could've cause that kind of scar, especially considering how long it was. The boy caught Beau staring and was prepared to snarl at him to get him to back off but paused when he saw Beau's expression. Beau just appeared to be genuinely curious.

"My name is Tobias," the vampire boy said at last and stuck his hand out cautiously towards Beau. Beau grinned and grabbed the boys hand and shook it firmly in his.

"That's a pretty interesting name," Beau remarked as he smiled back at Tobias. Tobias's mouth twitched up a bit at the corners, Beau's smile was contagious, and Tobias had to force the smile down that was about to come out on his face.

"Your name is pretty different as well, I hadn't heard of that name before," Tobias commented as he cocked his head to the side a bit, examining Beau like he was the first time that he had seen such a creature even though Tobias was the only real abnormal creature in the room. There was a stretch of silence as both the boys seemed to be taking in the fact that they were seeing each other this closely. A thought crossed Beau's mind that put a damper on his happy mood.

"I'm probably not going to see you again, am I?" Beau asked as he tried to keep his voice level, trying not to sound like he was too disappointed. He knew that Tobias had a family that he had to get back to and that he couldn't stay around in his little room forever. Tobias's face dropped a bit and he rubbed the back of his neck in thought.

"I mean it would be difficult, but I don't think that it would be impossible for us to meet again," Tobias replied after a bit of thinking. "But we'd have to meet somewhere other than here, its a bit too dangerous with all the other people around. Perhaps we could meet up at that old park down the street next Friday night. I mean you do seem pretty cool for a human, if not for the lack of your sense of danger."

Beau laughed, and Tobias just stared at him confused.

"That's probably the nicest thing that someone has ever said about me," Beau replied before continuing, "I'm not exactly considered cool by other humans, more like weird or a freak; I think that I've even been called a ghost and a witch at one point."

"Why is that?"

"Because I was born Albino I don't really have any colour pigments in my skin, so I appear very pale, and my eyes are a pale pink which has a tendency of freaking people out," Beau replied as he looked off to the left so that he wouldn't have to look Tobias in the eyes. Beau heard the shuffling as Tobias got closer to Beau and he could feel his cold slender fingers gently grip his chin and pulled it up so that he was looking directly at Tobias.

"They aren't freaky, they look beautiful, kind of like a sunrise," Tobias whispered in awe as he stared intently into Beau's eyes. "For the last 200 years I couldn't remember what it was like, I can't believe that I nearly forgotten the colours of a sunrise."

Beau was starting to turn a reddish-purple as he blushed, not used to hearing any kind of compliments from anyone other than Ms. Kay. But he glanced at Tobias curiously as he saw a deep sadness set in on his face.

"You really miss the sun that much, huh?" Beau asked trying to change the subject from the colour of his eyes.

"Yeah, I used to sneak out of our house just before dawn and watch the sun come up," Tobias replied as he chuckled to himself, seemingly lost in thought as he stared off at nothing smiling. "Well before I became this anyway, following the family tradition."

Beau noticed that Tobias seemed almost angry rather than sad when talking about how he had become a vampire; that the ideology of becoming a vampire ran in his family. Tobias got up from his crouch and waited for Beau to get up before he walked over to the window. Beau helped him to pull open the curtains and prop open the window. Tobias climbed up into the window and stuck his legs out the window before dropping off the ledge. Beau stuck his head out just in time to see Tobias come back up, floating in midair.

"Whoa," was all that Beau could manage to say as he watched Tobias floating in midair right in front of him. Tobias gave Beau a shy smile before he flew up and off, away from the house and out of Beau's sight.

Chapter 12

Beau woke up later than he usually did that next morning, and sleepily went through his usual morning routine without trying to get trampled by the other boys who were also rushing around trying to get dressed. Beau barely managed to avoid getting elbowed around as he brushed his hair and teeth before dodging bodies to get down the stairs. Beau yawned as he stepped off the stairs and into the kitchen, which immediately caught Ms. Kay's attention.

"Rough night?" Ms. Kay asked as she paused in her cooking to look over at Beau. Beau froze for a second and tried to think of a reason as to why he would still be so tired.

"I, uh, couldn't put this new book down until I had finished it," Beau replied quickly before jumping into setting up the kitchen table. He tried his best not to look at

Ms. Kay as he set the table, but he could feel her eyes on him. She knew that he was lying but he was sure that she wouldn't ask him about it, because what could she really say?

Beau had barely finished setting the table when a rush of hungry boys came down the stairs. Beau made sure to step out of the way and sat down at the only available seat once the other boys had settled down. Beau ate in his usual silence but squirmed a bit in his seat as he felt another pair of eyes on him. He glanced up from his food with a scowl on his face and saw that Kyle was now staring at him too with a concerned frown on his face. Beau frowned and tried to ignore Kyle as best as he could as he finished eating and got up to grab his stuff for school so that he could work on it in his room. As he was about to leave the kitchen Beau remembered that he needed to at least tell Ms. Kay something for next week so that she wouldn't be too suspicious about him leaving the house.

"Oh, my friend had to cancel for this weekend, but he wants to do a sleepover at his house next weekend if that's okay?" Beau asked as he stopped with one foot on the stairs and turned his body to half face Ms. Kay. She seemed surprised for second before slowly nodding her head. Beau's face broken out into a smile and he thanked her before running up the stairs to do his homework.

For the next couple days Beau started to notice that the things and people around him began to change, but mostly the people. Kyle had started trying to talk to him more and both him and Ms. Kay had started having private conversations in her study, which would stop once they knew that Beau was around. Beau had no idea what they were talking about, he just knew that it had something to do with him.

Besides the suspicion that he was being discussed behind his back, Beau was excited for the arrival of Friday. He couldn't wait to be able to see Tobias again, but he was also afraid that Tobias might back out and just leave him stranded at the park. He wasn't really all that nervous about Tobias himself, which he knew that he probably should've been considering that Tobias was a vampire after all.

When Friday finally arrived, Beau was anxious to get home from school, a bundle of excited nerves twisted and flipped in his stomach. He hadn't been this excited to do something and go somewhere new in a long time, usually too busy with his nose in his newest book to really want to do anything that he didn't think was more than just interesting.

On the bus ride home Beau kept tapping his foot on the floor of the bus, full of nervous energy and excitement. When he had finally arrived at his stop he practically ran off the bus and down the street to the boys' home. Beau ran in the front door of the house before calming down so that he didn't draw unwanted attention to himself. He was about to walk up the stairs to his room when he heard someone say his name from the study. It was too quiet for someone to have been trying to call him, someone must be talking about him.

Curious, Beau inched closer to the study so that he could hear better. Beau knew that the voices were Kyle and Ms. Kay, and he was only being able to catch snippets of what they were saying. It was something along the lines of contacting an outside source to get rid of a problem that was surrounding Beau, but they were both hesitant to do so. Beau walked away from the door before either of them decided to come out. He walked up the stairs to his room and packed a small bag of stuff so that it would look like he was going out to an actual sleepover.

Beau tried to do some homework to past the time until dusk, but he was too excited to focus, already forgetting about hearing about Kyle and the Ms. Kay's conversation. Kyle came into Beau's room at about 7 o'clock as Beau was just finishing up packing a couple more things into his bag. Beau tried his best to just ignore him, but Kyle came right up to him and sat down next to him on the floor, reaching for the bag. Beau pulled the bag back away from him as he glared at Kyle.

"What do you want?" Beau asked as he zipped up the bag and through it over his shoulders so that it settled comfortably on his back. Beau was starting to get really annoyed with all the overprotective attention that he was getting from Kyle, who used to want nothing to do with him.

"I was just going to check to make sure that you hadn't forgotten anything," Kyle replied with his arms raised in surrender. "But if you think that you have everything than alright I won't interfere."

Beau got up from the floor and left the room, leaving Kyle to sit in the room by himself. Beau walked down the stairs to say goodbye to Ms. Kay, who was on the phone in the kitchen. She smiled when she saw him and held a hand of the bottom part of the phone as she whispered, "have fun". Beau smiled back and walked out the front door of the house, and towards the park. The sun had almost completely set by the time he had gotten to the park. He decided to play on the swing set and the jungle gym for a bit as he waited for the sun to set and for Tobias to show up.

As the sun set on the horizon, creating a glow of reds and oranges before going to navy and then black, Beau thought back to what Tobias had said about him loving the sunrise. Beau realized that he was a bit of the opposite, he loved the night. The twinkling of the stars on a clear night and the ever bright and ever-changing moon moving gracefully across the sky. Beau laid on his back on a ramp in the jungle gym and stared up at the sky as the stars started to come out.

After a few minutes, Beau started to wonder if Tobias was ever going to show up at all; maybe he was the only one that was looking forward to hanging out again. Beau sighed and laid there for a few more minutes. He was about to give up and go home when he heard a light thud coming from the railing that was just above his head.

Beau glanced backwards towards the noise and smiled when he saw in the dim light of the night Tobias perched up on the railing with one leg dangling just behind Beau's head. Tobias was smiling down at Beau before hopping off the railing to join him on the ramp of the jungle gym.

Chapter 13

Beau giggled as he ran across the top ramp of the jungle gym and after Tobias, who was now on the ground at the bottom of the stairs of the jungle gym. Beau chased after Tobias as they both ran across the playground laughing. Tobias jumped from the ground in front of the jungle gym to the top railing on the top of the jungle gym. Beau's mouth dropped open at the sheer height that Tobias had scaled with just one jump. He quickly recovered from his shock and smiled up at Tobias before scaling the slide to get back up onto the jungle gym.

Tobias watched with intrigued eyes as Beau clamber his way up the slide and back onto the ramp. Panting as he stood with a smile on his face in front of Tobias. Tobias smiled back but was still studying Beau as if he were the most interesting creature that he had ever seen. He had not expected Beau to be so accepting of what he was and still be so adventurous.

"What?" Beau asked as he raised an eyebrow at Tobias, his staring was making him a bit uncomfortable as it was more like a predatory stare rather than a quizzical stare.

"Let's go play on the swings," Tobias said as he jumped from the railing and landed next to the swing set. Tobias waited patiently, leaning against the swing set, for Beau to catch up with him. Beau slid down the slide before running over to where Tobias was standing next to the swings. When Beau caught up to Tobias they both walked over and picked a swing to swing on and swung in a contented silence for a few minutes. Tobias glanced over at Beau, seeing his contented face but also noticing his slow dropping in body temperature. Tobias couldn't feel the cold and for a moment had forgotten that Beau still could. He knew that Beau wouldn't probably last too much longer out there on the playground with him already starting to shiver slightly in the light breeze.

"Hey, did you maybe want to come over to my house to play for a bit?" Tobias asked grinning, looking expectantly at Beau.

Beau planted his feet on the ground, immediately stopping his swinging motion, but still hesitated in his response to Tobias. Did he really want to go walking into a vampire's lair with this vampire boy? Did Beau really trust Tobias enough to walk right into such a dangerous place?

Tobias noticing Beau's hesitation quickly added that he would make sure that nothing would happen to Beau while he was at the house as his guest.

"My family is out hunting and won't be back for a few hours, so it'll be safe for you to come down for a bit to hang out if you like; it'll be warmer than staying out here," Tobias reassured Beau but then gestured to Beau as he mentioned the part about it being warmer than staying out on the playground. Beau shivered slightly in the chilly night air as he smiled shyly while rubbing his arms to try to keep them warm.

"Well that does sound better than me catching a cold," Beau replied shyly, slightly embarrassed, but after a moment his eyebrows scrunched up together in confusion. "But how are we supposed to get there? Is it close enough that we can walk there?"

Tobias chuckled before shaking his head no to Beau's question before explaining the only way that they were going to be able to make it to Tobias's house.

"No, we are going to have to fly there, it's on the outskirts of town away from prying eyes," Tobias replied as he held his hand out in Beau's direction. Beau stared at Tobias for a moment, curious as to what he was talking about and why he had offered his hand to Beau. Beau hesitantly took Tobias's cold hand in his and smiled nervously at him. Tobias quickly pulled Beau to his chest with a mischievous look in his eyes and a smile plastered on his face, before launching himself towards the sky with Beau wrapped tightly in his arms.

Beau squeezed his eyes shut as panic began to sink in and he gripped tightly on to Tobias's leather jacket. Tobias chuckled to himself before leveling out when he thought that they were high enough above the city.

"Its okay, you can open your eyes now," Tobias called loudly over the rushing sound of the wind. Beau nervously cracked open one of his eyes and turned his head to the side to try to look down at the world that was behind him, that was hundreds of miles down. Beau gasped and tightened his grip on Tobias but couldn't take his eyes off the tiny city that seemed to be floating on far below him. It was beautiful and terrifying...kind of like Tobias.

Soon the houses and city lights started to dim and dwindle, until there was nothing left but an evergreen forest and a dirt road that cut through a small section of the forest. After a few minutes had passed Beau began to shiver again, much harder this time around, and being as close as he was to Tobias, who was naturally cold, didn't really help his case. Tobias started a slow descent so that they were now just above the treetops, that's when Beau spotted it. Nestled in a grove of trees not too far away was the biggest house he had ever seen.

"Wow," was all that Beau could manage to think of saying when the entire house came into view.

"I suppose it is pretty nice, but it can feel like a bit of a prison at times," Tobias commented as he tried his best to speak over the rushing noise of the wind, sounding a bit sad even to Beau's untrained ears. "Sometimes we aren't allowed to leave the house for days on end, it can be very suffocating."

Beau looked up at Tobias's face and saw that it had hardened to not the usual smiling face that Beau had started to get to know well. Tobias seemed very serious and it looked very unnatural on his face, at least from Beau's perspective it seemed unnatural. It concerned Beau to see Tobias react in such a quick and darkening manner. Beau could even feel Tobias tighten his grip around Beau's waist to the point that it was slightly painful. Beau grunted in pain and Tobias face relaxed as he looked down at Beau, loosening his grip so that it wasn't painfully tight around Beau's waist.

Tobias pulled them upright as they began their descent to the front of the Victorian styled mansion that had a large stone fountain in the middle of the driveway. The fountain looked to be a three-tiered marble fountain rather than the regular stone that Beau had first thought it would be.

"Well, here we are, home sweet home," Tobias said as he lowered Beau and himself onto the ground just in front of the fountain. Beau could hear a bit of bitterness in Tobias's voice as he had said that, and was curious as to what could be so bad about having a place to come back to, about having a real family? Tobias noticed Beau staring at him with a questioning expression on his face. Instead of responding though, Tobias just gave a tired smile and started walking towards the house. Beau quickly hurried behind Tobias, not wanting to be left on his own at a vampire family's house.

Chapter 14

Beau hurried up the stone steps behind Tobias, doing his best to keep up with Tobias's steady yet rapid steps. At the top of the large stone staircase that led up to the house was two large dark wooden doors that towered over the both of them. There was no knocker on the door or even any handles, but it still opened, like magic, when they both approached the door. Beau knew that the house was massive just by the shadowy view that he got of it amongst the trees but once he saw the inside, Beau knew immediately that it was much bigger than he had first anticipated.

When Tobias and Beau walked in the front door they were greeted by a grand foyer with a tiled floor and a carpet that went from the doorway all the way to the stairs that were at the other end of the hall. There was a twin set of stairs that went up to the same second floor landing, kind of like the staircase in the movie Gone with the Wind, but bigger and made entirely of marble with the same red satin carpet covering the middle of stairs, disappearing out of view at the top step.

A huge crystal chandelier hung in the middle of the grand foyer, with paintings of landscapes lining the walls. Beau could vaguely see at the top of the stairs more paintings, but those more closely resembled portraits. The paintings were a bit difficult to make out at this distance for Beau, so he stuck to looking at the things that were closer to him.

Beau kept his pace next to Tobias as he scanned the room in wonder and amazement with a huge grin on his face. Tobias glanced back at Beau every so often with a small smile on his face as he saw Beau's reactions. Tobias felt something stir in his cold dead heart as he watched Beau, it felt uncomfortable but not unwanted. Tobias had been paying so much attention to Beau that he stopped paying attention to his surroundings for a moment, caught up in something that must've been bliss for it to have felt that good.

When Beau froze at the base of stairs, staring up at something at the top of the stairs Tobias immediately went into protective mode. Tobias jumped in front of Beau with his claws out and snarled, with bared fangs, up at the person that was at the top of the stairs. Tobias quickly straightened up when he realized who it was that was standing at the top of the stairs.

"Mortimer, sorry about that, I didn't realize that it was you," Tobias commented bashfully as he twiddled with his fingers, opening and closing his fists nervously at his sides. Mortimer was a middle aged looking man who was wearing a black tuxedo with tails on the jacket, and a white shirt underneath, he looked very much like a butler.

"Its alright Young Master, but I do believe that some introductions are in order," Mortimer replied smiling ruefully at Tobias. Tobias looked to his side for Beau, but he didn't see him. Tobias felt a shot panic until he felt Beau's hands tightly gripped the back of his leather jacket. Tobias looked underneath his arm and saw Beau peek out from behind him, staring fearfully up at Mortimer.

"Beau this is Mortimer, he's one of the humans that lives in the house," Tobias said as he stepped aside a bit to make Beau more visible to Mortimer. "Mortimer this Beau, he's my new friend, and he's also a human."

"I see, and do your parents know that he's here?" Mortimer asked as he eyed Beau with a raised eyebrow. Tobias knew that he was in dangerous waters now, but he wasn't about to back down when it came to protecting Beau from his own parents, even if that meant that he had to stand up to Mortimer.

"No, and I'll make sure that it stays that way, no matter what," Tobias remarked with a hostile tone as he bared his fangs back at Mortimer again, this time with the full intent to intimidate him. Then Tobias grabbed Beau's wrist and led him away down to a door that was just to the left of the stairs. Gently encouraging Beau to go through the door with Tobias's reassuring hand on the middle of his back.

"Are you sure that its okay for me to be here?" Beau asked nervously as he watched Tobias close the door behind them. Tobias gave a tired smile to Beau before leading him further down the hallway with a hand on his back again.

"Yeah, it'll be fine, don't worry about it," Tobias replied trying to change the subject, so that he wouldn't have to lie to Beau. He was nervous that Beau would question him further on his lack of response but was grateful when Beau just nodded instead.

"I am curious though, why is there a human in your house?" Beau asked as he glanced over to Tobias as they walked down the hallway. Not a complete change of subject but Tobias could deal with it.

"He's one of what my family like to call Blood Sheep, they are humans that we keep around the house to make it appear lived in during the day," Tobias explained as he dropped his hand from Beau's back and instead put his hands into his front pockets. "We also feed off them if it's too dangerous to hunt that night or if one of us is too weak to hunt a certain night due to whatever circumstances. Mortimer is mainly my mother's Blood Sheep, though occasionally she will feed off the others. But there is something that I want to show you before I must take you back home, follow me!"

Tobias took off down the hallway with a grin on his face, making sure not to go too fast that he would lose Beau. They passed more paintings like the ones in the foyer and some older expensive looking vases that were seated on white stone pedestals. Eventually, Tobias stopped in front of a set of large oak double doors. He gave a mischievous smile to Beau before opening the doors without another word. Beau stared wide eyed at the biggest library he had ever seen in his entire short life. He turned to look at Tobias whose smile had wavered slightly after not really getting any kind of reaction from Beau. Beau broke out into the biggest smile before grabbing Tobias's hand and dragging him into the library with him, letting the door close behind them.

Chapter 15

It was around 3 o'clock in the morning when Beau started to get very sleepy while sitting in the library trying to read a really good book, in an older styled leather chair. He yawned and rubbed his eyes with one hand as the other held the book open on his lap. Beau heard a quiet whoosh and looked up as he saw Tobias hovering in mid-air just in front of the railing. Beau was reading on the third-floor balcony of the library, making for a long climb up the stairs, well if there had been any stairs. The only way that Beau had managed to get up there was with Tobias flying him up there.

"Are you okay?" Tobias asked as he floated over the railing before landing on the floor of the balcony a couple feet away from where Beau was curled up in the large armchair. Beau nodded slowly as he yawned again before laying his head on his arm which was laying across the arm of the comfy chair, forgetting the book that was resting in his lap.

"Just getting...really sleepy," Beau replied quietly as he gave a tired smile to Tobias, his eyes only lazily half open as he stared at Tobias. The only thing that Beau's sleep hazy mind could think of as he stared at Tobias was that he didn't want to leave; he just wanted to snuggle up and sleep for the rest of the night. But he was doing his best to stay awake for Tobias's sake since Beau was having such a fun time hanging out with him.

"If you want you can take the book back with you and then just bring it back the next time that you come up here," Tobias offered with a small smile, having nearly forgotten that humans need to have some sleep at night. Beau opened his mouth to thank Tobias but frowned as he thought about how he would explain such an old book being in his possession.

"I think that I may just have to come back here to finish reading it," Beau replied as he stood up from the chair and stretched. "It may turn some heads if I were to bring it back with me, and I don't want it to get ruined if the wrong person were to get a hold of it."

Tobias's smile faltered for a moment but then he nodded his head in understanding. The only thing was, was that he really didn't understand, at least not everything that Beau was thinking about. Beau knew that something weird was going on at the boys' home and he didn't want Tobias to get mixed up in that.

"I promise that I will come and hang out again though, how about we do another 'sleepover' next Friday?" Beau asked as he put the word sleepover into air quotations as he smiled at Tobias. Tobias chuckled at Beau's half-asleep attempt at humour. "I'll finish the book then, that sound okay?"

"Yeah, that sounds great," Tobias replied as he led Beau over to the edge of the railing. Tobias got up onto the railing before stepping off, dropping down a couple feet before floating back up to get Beau. Beau got up onto the railing, throwing his legs over the top of the railing so that they dangled dangerous over the probably deadly drop. Tobias reached his hand out to Beau, who took it, and pushed himself off the metal railing as Tobias pulled him against himself. They both slowly descended to the floor of the library, Beau trying his best to stay awake in Tobias's arms but nearly failing. Beau only startled awake when his feet touched the floor.

On the way out of Tobias's house there was a bit more noise then the silence that Beau had first arrived in, even though it was still eerily quiet compared to what it was like back home. When Beau had finally arrived back home he had nearly fallen asleep again on the flight with Tobias back to the boys' home.

Upon arrival Beau had this reluctant feeling about saying goodbye to Tobias, he hadn't felt this connected to a person...ever. It was unnerving to Beau but also comforting to know that he had someone else there that he could fully trust. Tobias seemed to be hesitating to leave as well, shifting slowly from foot to foot as he looked at Beau with a shy smile. He wasn't too sure what to say or do as he felt kind of awkward to just stand there.

"Well...umm...I guess that I will see you next Friday than," Tobias murmured as he rubbed the back of his head. Beau nodded silently as he looked to Tobias, neither of them moving from their spot a couple houses down from the boys' home. Both

Tobias and Beau didn't really want to separate but they both knew that they had to, at the very least for Tobias's sake as the sun would be starting to come up soon.

"You better get going before the sun comes up," Beau mentioned as he gestured vaguely with his arm to the lightening horizon. Tobias glanced back towards the horizon before sighing, dejectedly.

"Yeah, I suppose, then see you later my Răsărit[1]," Tobias murmured before raising Beau's right hand to his lips. After kissing Beau's hand Tobias took off towards the sky, heading back towards his home which was feeling more and more like a prison the further that Tobias got away from Beau.

Beau stood there for a moment in stunned silence staring after where Tobias had taken off to, before looking back down at his right hand. Beau's legs felt like jelly and his mind was all fuzzy. He smacked himself on his cheeks to try to wake himself up out of his daze, then he took off running towards the boys' home. He stopped on the sidewalk just outside the house to catch his

---

[1] Răsărit means Sunrise in Romanian

breath, so that he wouldn't make a lot of noise when he walked into the house.

As Beau walked up the steps to the boys' home there was something out of the corner of his eye that caught his attention. He looked up to the side of the house and squinted in the low light at a small red dot that flashed on and off in a slow rhythmic motion. The dark silhouette that had the red dot on it looked like a vaguely familiar kind of shape. It took a couple more moments for Beau to figure out that the silhouette was that of a video surveillance camera that was aimed at the front door...and part of the street in the direction where Beau had just come from.

As Beau stared at it with his head cocked to the side as he wondered why he had never noticed that camera being there before. He pushed that thought to the back of his mind as he focused on staying as quiet as he could as he unlocked the front door of the boys' home and squeezed inside, locking it behind himself. Thinking to himself that he must've just over looked the camera the last time that he had come home so late at night.

He snuck upstairs to his bedroom and tucked himself into bed, trying to be as quiet as he possibly could. Quickly drifting off to sleep as soon as he pulled the blankets up around his neck, with a smile on his face as he dreamed about that night.

Chapter 16

Beau woke up late Saturday morning, enjoying being able to get to sleep in a bit more for a change. The only reason why he woke up though, and didn't sleep in longer like he had wanted, was because Kyle had loudly strutted into the room practically stomping his feet the entire time.

Beau groaned and rolled over so that he was now facing the wall and doing his best to ignore Kyle's presence. But Kyle was not about to let Beau ignore him and walked over to the curtains pulling them open in one smooth movement. Beau groaned even louder in protest and pulled the blankets up over his head, hiding from the bright sunlight.

"Come on now, you aren't going to stay in bed all day," Kyle grumbled as he grabbed the bottom edge of the blankets and yanked them off Beau, dropping the blankets onto the floor at his feet.

Beau slowly sat up and glared daggers at Kyle as he stood at the end of the bed, leaning onto one of the bunk bed posts. Kyle had a smug smirk on his face as he crossed his arms over his chest. Beau knew that there was no chance of him going back to bed now, so he staggered to his feet and left the room without another glance back to Kyle. But Kyle wasn't done talking to Beau yet. Kyle quickly caught up to Beau with a few short jogging strides and was now walking beside him down the hallway.

"So, what did you guys do last night?" Kyle asked as he kept pace next to Beau. "You look like death; did you and your friend not sleep at all last night at the sleepover?"

"We both share a love of reading, so we were both up late reading last night," Beau snapped as he stopped at the top of the stairs. "Something that a person like you wouldn't understand!"

Beau had no idea what had made him so cranky, whether it was from the lack of sleep or the fact that Kyle had suddenly decided to become super chummy with him after nearly a year of bullying. Either way, Beau wanted nothing to do with whatever Kyle was trying to do, especially not after hearing snippets of his conversation with Ms. Kay. Talking about his new friend to Kyle just didn't seem like the smartest idea.

Beau turned his head and walked down the stairs without a backwards glance to Kyle. When Beau entered the kitchen, he took one of the two remaining at the far end of the table and silently put some food onto his plate. He tried not to look at Kyle when he came to sit at the table, and instead just focused on his plate and vaguely listening into the other boys' conversations.

After having eaten a bit of his breakfast, Beau had managed to calm down a bit. As he thought about the fun time that he had had at Tobias's house, his mood started to perk up a bit. Beau even managed to smile to himself as he thought about going to visit Tobias's house again the next Friday. Maybe Beau should bring something to do for the next time. He wondered if Tobias liked fishing or if he even knew how to fish considering his probable age and rich lifestyle. That would be a fun thing that they could do together if Tobias wanted to try it.

"So, how was the sleepover at your friend's house?" Ms. Kay asked, drawing Beau's attention for the first time since he had entered the kitchen.

Beau looked down to where she sat at the other end of the table, noticing that she was staring at him expectantly. Beau took a quick bite of his food so that he had a moment to think before he responded to her question. He couldn't really say too much, but he knew that he wouldn't be able to lie to her either.

"It was fun," Beau replied with his best smile, hoping that she wouldn't ask anything more but knowing that she probably would. Beau was surprised when Ms. Kay just smiled and nodded her head before going back to eating her own food. He stared quizzically at his own food before taking another bite. He had been sure that she was going to ask more than just that about his stay at his new friend's house, whom she had never met. Kind of like what Kyle had been trying to do upstairs, with him asking questions and sticking to Beau's side like a bee to honey.

Beau couldn't let his own suspicions dampen his mood, he was far too excited about his next visit to Tobias's house to think too much about what was really going on around him. But he knew that there was something that was very off going on in the house behind closed doors.

Chapter 17

"Wait, what do you mean I can't go?" Beau asked as he dropped the dish that he was washing back into the sink. "You've been on me about making friends and hanging out with people my own age, and now you won't even let me do just that?"

"Beau, that's not what this is about," Ms. Kay said as she put a couple plates away in the upper cupboards. "All the other boys have chores too, so this isn't just about you."

"But I've done all my chores already and I had asked you three days ago if I could go out tonight," Beau complained as he washed up a couple more dishes and put them on the drying rack.

"You still have to finish cleaning up the kitchen and clean your room," Ms. Kay said as she stared at Beau, and for a second

Beau thought that he had seen something scary lurking in her eyes. Ms. Kay smiled, ridding her face of the dark shadow, and patted Beau on the head. Maybe he had just been seeing things or misinterpreted something when he had been looking at her. "As soon as you finish all of that stuff then you can go and spend the night at your friend's place, alright?"

"Alright," Beau grumbled as he finished washing up the last of the dishes that were in the sink from dinner. As Beau went about cleaning the kitchen, he kept glancing out of the corner of his eye at the setting sun outside the front window. He bit his lower lip and sped up his cleaning effort so that he wouldn't leave Tobias wondering what had happened to him or if Beau had just decided not to show up.

When Beau had finally managed to get the approval of Ms. Kay that the kitchen was indeed clean, he excused himself upstairs to quickly clean up the room that he shared. When Beau walked into the room his mouth dropped open, he slapped his hand on his forehead, and groaned. The room looked like a tornado had hit it, clothes and toys were strewn all over the place, and the beds were a mess.

Beau sighed, rolled up his sleeves, and started to clean up the room, picking up whatever was closest to him first. If he didn't know any better, he would've said that they had done this on purpose because no one makes a mess this big just by accident. But since he knew that these boys could get messy he really didn't think too much of the disaster.

When he was finally finished cleaning the room to the approval of Ms. Kay, the sun had already set, and darkness had settled over the sky. Beau was starting to feel a bit disheartened that Tobias might not still be at the park when he got there. Beau hopped from foot to foot as Ms. Kay slowly inspected the last parts of the room.

"Looks like you're off the hook," Ms. Kay said as she walked back to where Beau stood in the doorway of the room. "Alright, go and have fun at your friend's house, but please make sure to be safe, there are all kinds of people wandering around the streets at night."

"Yes ma'am!" Beau replied excitedly as he gave her a quick hug before grabbed the backpack from his bed and practically ran out of the room and down the stairs. He paused at the door to put on some shoes and noticed Kyle standing in the doorway to Ms. Kay's study, watching him with a conflicted look as Beau got ready to leave.

Beau mentally shook himself and focused on the task of getting his shoes on. As soon as they were firmly on his feet, he threw open the door, and tried not to slam it close as he took off towards the park. Beau ran as fast as his feet would carry him all the way to the park without stopping for a moment to breathe. When he had finally arrived at the park he was panting heavily and had to stop just in front of the park, bent over with his hands on his knees.

"I was afraid that you weren't going to show up," a voice said from somewhere above Beau's head. Beau turned his head to the side, looked up, and saw Tobias with his hands in his lap sitting on the wall that surrounded the playground. He was smiling down at Beau, but he looked very relieved, and for a moment Beau forgot that Tobias was a probably a very old and dangerous vampire. Beau stood up straight and smiled, walking quickly over to Tobias. He stopped when he was right next to Tobias's legs so that he could lean on the wall while he finished catching his breath.

"Sorry, I had a little trouble getting out of the house," Beau said as he placed his hands on the wall and looked over into the dark playground. It always looked so much spookier at night when there was no one around.

Beau heard a weird sound coming from right below his right ear, close to his neck. It confused him because it wasn't all that windy out, in fact, it kind of sounded like an animal was sniffing his neck. Beau slowly turned his head to look at Tobias and saw something in his eyes for just a second before he pulled back and put some space between them faster than Beau could blink. But what he had seen in Tobias's eyes was not anything like a normal human, it was dark, and it was predatory.

"S-sorry," Tobias said quickly as he stared down at the ground, the blue veins in his cheeks and neck growing more pronounced. The only reason that Beau could think of for that was the fact that Tobias might have been embarrassed. *Could that seriously be his version of blushing?* "I haven't eaten in a few days, and you just...well...you just smell really good."

Beau knew at that point that he should've been afraid, that he should've run as far away from Tobias as he could. But he didn't heed the warnings that were going off in his head and instead closed the distance that Tobias had put between them and rested a hand on Tobias's leg, drawing his attention back to Beau.

"Have you ever been fishing?" Beau asked suddenly, causing Tobias to raise an eyebrow and cock his head to the side.

"Can't say that I have, we usually had servants go and fetch the fish from the market," Tobias replied as he stared towards the sky, watching the stars, veins popping in his neck and cheeks again. Beau wasn't really thinking about how the closeness of him to Tobias was affecting Tobias's self control.

"Would you like to learn?" Beau asked trying not to look too excited, but he was pretty sure that he was failing at it, not that he cared. Though he was completely oblivious to Tobias's pains as he sat next to Beau trying not to breathe in too deeply. Even then, Tobias could still see that this meant a lot to Beau especially considering that when he was like this the different colours in his eyes became more prominent than usual.

"Alright, sure! There's a pond that's not too far away from my house if you want to go there?" Tobias said as he leaned down closer to Beau, trying to test his resolve since he knew he would have to fly Beau all the way back to his house. Beau grinned and held out his hand towards Tobias, completely oblivious. Tobias pulled Beau up onto the wall as he stood up and, with his arms wrapped around Beau's waist and Beau's arms wrapped around his neck, they took off towards Tobias's house.

Chapter 18

They could see the house from the air as they approached it, but Tobias flew them just beyond the house and into a clearing in the forest behind the house. As Tobias lowered them to the ground, Beau noticed that they were in a large garden that extended to the treelines on either side. In the middle of the garden there was a large white gazebo that was covered in leafy vines and that had some lit lanterns glowing from a couple different spots inside the gazebo.

Beau turned to Tobias to ask about the gazebo, but Tobias started dragging Beau away into the forest before he was able to say anything. Tobias made sure that he went slow enough that Beau was able to keep up without hurting himself. When Tobias finally stopped running, Beau was panting heavily and had to sit down for a moment to catch his breath.

"Are...Are we there yet?" Beau asked between breaths as he collapsed backwards onto the grass so that he was lying down. The cool grass feeling nice on his overheated flesh from all the running that he had done that day.

"Yep, its right over here," Tobias replied as he pointed between two trees where a couple large rocks poked out of the ground, the roots of the trees having grown around them probably many years ago.

Beau got back up to his feet and went to stand next to Tobias. As Beau looked out between the trees he was surprised to see such clear water right at the base of the rocks; spreading all the way out to some smallish looking black smudges in the distance. The pond appeared almost magical as the moonlight reflected off the water, creating a sparkling scene of light and dark.

"Wow, this place is amazing, I had no idea that this kind of place was even back here," Beau commented in awe as he stared out at the large body of water from his perch on the rocks with Tobias standing on the ground just behind him. This did not look like a pond at all, it was far too big, but maybe this was a pond in Tobias's eyes considering the house that he lived in and everything. Tobias couldn't help but smile as he watched Beau admire the scenery by the moonlight.

"So, how exactly does this fishing thing work?" Tobias asked drawing Beau's attention back to him.

"Hmm? Oh right!" Beau exclaimed as he jumped down from the rock and slung his backpack off his back and dropped it onto the ground. Beau quickly unzipped the bag and pulled out the dismembered fishing rod that he had brought with him. Beau began to put the fishing rod back together as he could hear Tobias slowly approach him from behind. Beau put the last couple pieces together as Tobias leaned down over Beau's shoulder, staring curiously at the strange contraption in Beau's hands.

"What's that?" Tobias asked, his voice right next to Beau's ear sending a weird chill down Beau's spine.

"Um, this is a fishing rod, it's what we are going to use to catch the fish," Beau explained once he had recovered himself.

"How?" Tobias asked doubtfully as he stood back up to his full height and crossed his arms.

"I'll show you," Beau said as he walked back over to the rocks. He checked over his shoulder to make sure that Tobias wasn't in the way, then swung the fishing line back before thrusting it forward about 3 metres away into the water. He sat down on the rock and patted the rock next to him as he glanced over his shoulder to Tobias. Tobias took the seat next to Beau and stared at the spot where the little white and red bobber was floating in the water a few metres away.

"Now what?" Tobias asked curiously, as he watched the red and white bobber sway with the ripples of the water.

"Now we wait for the fish to take the bait, which is when that little white and red floater gets pulled under the water," Beau explained as he pointed to the bobber that Tobias had been staring at intently.

"How long will that take?" Tobias asked as he sat forward on his hands, leaning out over the water staring intently at the white and red floater.

"I don't really know," Beau replied as he put a finger to his chin in thought. "I have been told that you do need a lot of patience for this though."

"Ohh," Tobias commented as he sat back on the rock normally. As Tobias sat on the rock next to Beau the longer that he waited the more fidgety he got. Tobias tried his best to stay as still as he could but sitting still was never one of his fortes, even when he had been a human. His father had always said that he needed to learn to be able to be patient, when it came to both hunting and his private schooling.

"Sorry, I know that it's not the most active thing to do," Beau commented as he noticed Tobias's fidgeting out of the corner of his eye.

"No, no, don't worry about that I need to practise sitting still and being patient, so this is good for me," Tobias said as he smiled reassuringly at Beau, then some motion out of the corner of his eye caught Tobias's attention. "The floating thing just went under the water!"

"Did you want to reel it in?" Beau asked as he started to pull back on the rod to make sure that there really was a fish on the line, it sure felt like it to him.

"Can I?" Tobias asked excitedly as he looked at Beau to make sure that he was being serious.

"Yeah!" Beau replied and handed the rod over to Tobias as Beau slid down the rock and the dirt that dropped off into the cold water of the pond below him. The water went up to just above his ankles and soaked through his shoes. "Now just slowly wind up the string using that crank on the side of the rod and lean back a bit."

"Like this?" Tobias asked as he leaned back on the rock and started to reel the fish in towards them.

"Yeah that's perfect! I'll stay down here and pull the fish out of the water so that we can see what we managed to catch."

"Okay!"

Beau waited bent over with his hands hovering over the water as he watched Tobias reel the line closer and closer to the shore. Beau took a couple steps closer to the fishing line that was making ripples in the water and waited as the line was only a couple feet away from him. Then Beau dove for the fish, splashing water all over himself as he grabbed for the line and the fish's mouth.

"Got it!" Beau called back up to Tobias once he had a firm grip on the large fish's mouth. Beau felt a presence just above his shoulder and looked up to see Tobias floating upside down just above his shoulder. Beau nearly wound up knocking heads with Tobias because of how close he had gotten when he had floated down.

"Wow, so what are we supposed to do with it now that we caught it?" Tobias as he stared the large fish with excitement and wonder. It wasn't like he had never seen a fish before, but this was a very different way than what he was used to seeing fish like. Usually the fish came in already cooked and on special dinner platters.

"Sometimes people like to cook the fish and eat it, but tonight I think that we are just going to let him go," Beau replied as he carefully took the hook out of the fish's mouth before letting him go back into the water. The fish was still for a moment and then took off like a bullet out of a gun, disappearing back into the water. "And that is how you fish."

"That's so cool!" Tobias said excitedly as he turned his body in the air so that he was looking directly at Beau with his feet hovering just above the water.

"Really?" Beau asked not completely convinced as he remember how much

Tobias had fidgeted while they were waiting to catch the fish.

"Yeah really, but your kind of all wet now," Tobias said as he looked at Beau's clothes. "Did you maybe want to go sit by the gazebo to see if you dry off a bit? It'll probably be a bit better than just sitting by the water in soaking wet clothes. Plus, we could probably hang some of the wet clothes up on the railings of the gazebo."

"Yeah sure, anything sounds better than just sitting in these wet clothes," Beau replied as he tugged at his wet shirt. Tobias held his hand down to Beau and gently lifted him back up onto the rocks. They started walking back towards the garden where Beau had first seen the beautiful white gazebo when they had arrived.

Chapter 19

Arriving back to the beautiful flower garden that they had first seen when they had arrived at Tobias's house. Now that Beau was finally able to look at it without being dragged off into the woods by Tobias, he could really see that there was a lot of effort put in to making this garden look so immaculately beautiful.

The delicate flower blossoms, though closed for the night, were each placed in their own section on the garden so that they were not meshing with any of the other colourful flowers that were around them. There were small trenches around the dirt flower beds that separated each of them from the grass and one large willow tree that stood just behind the glowing white gazebo.

As Beau and Tobias approached the gazebo, Beau was able to see that there were benches built into the white wooden rails that went around the entire circular gazebo. It kind of looked like one of those older Victorian styled round gazebos, but it looked like it had just been freshly painted maybe a few days ago.

Besides the benches that were in the gazebo the only other thing that was in the gazebo furniture wise was what looked to be a built-up fire pit that looked much more modern than the gazebo did. The fire pit was made from a solid white stone, that looked like it could've been marble, that stood roughly two feet tall in the middle of the gazebo.

Beau walked up the steps of the gazebo just behind Tobias. Tobias went and took a seat on a bench that was just off to the left of the stairs. That's when Beau realized that there were colourful striped cushions on the seats, and he was reminded as to how wet his t-shirt was. He did not want to ruin the cushions with his wet shirt, so he did as Tobias had mentioned on the way back to the garden and took his shirt off. Beau carefully hung the shirt over the railing that was just behind the bench that he was going to sit on with Tobias.

Beau was happy though that he hadn't gotten his pants too wet when he had dove for the fish, that would've been a more embarrassing situation to have to deal with. Luckily the parts of the pants that had gotten wet had pretty much completely dried on the walk back through the forest.

Beau sat down on the bench just as Tobias got up and walked over to the big fire pit that was standing in the middle of the floor of the gazebo. Beau stared at Tobias with scrunched up eyebrows as he watched him go up to the fire place and pick up a box that Beau hadn't noticed was sitting on the top of the fire pit. Beau couldn't see what Tobias was doing but after a moment or two Tobias came back to the bench and sat down. Beau looked back over to the fire pit and noticed that there was a fire now burning brightly from the top, making Beau feel warmer as he sat on the bench in just his shorts.

"Thanks," Beau said to Tobias as he smiled over to him, splaying his hands out towards the fire.

"No problem," Tobias replied as he smiled back, but Beau noticed that Tobias had this puzzled look on his face.

"What? Is something wrong?"

"No, but I am curious about something if you don't mind me asking."

"Sure, I don't mind, you can ask me anything."

"What's the scar on your eye from?"

Beau hesitated for a moment, not too sure how he should explain it since he himself didn't really know that had happened. The only thing that he knew was what Ms. Kay had told him, but even she had said that she didn't know too much.

"I'm not really sure because it had happened when I was a baby," Beau replied as he looked to Tobias and gingerly touched at the different texture of the scar on his eye. "What I've been told though is that I got it from an accident that had happened to my mother and I had been too close, so I had gotten hit too. I'm not too sure what by though because Ms. Kay said that she had found me in a cardboard box behind a big green garbage bin in the alleyway next to her apartment."

"That's rather strange," Tobias said as he pulled a leg up onto the bench and rested his head on his knee. "I don't know how anyone could ever abandon you, because I really like hanging out with you.

Though I don't know how much longer we are going to be able to do it."

"Why do you think that?" Beau asked noticing the saddening of Tobias's eyes and his slumped shoulders. The thought of never being able to hang out with Tobias again was not something that he had ever thought would happen.

"I'm engaged to a younger female vampire, even though she looks a lot older than me," Tobias replied with a growl, not meeting Beau's eyes. "My father thinks that because I'm 200 years old that if I haven't found my life mate by now than I won't ever, so he arranged this with another well-off family. There is a rather large problem with this kind of thing though, which is why arranged marriages are usually frowned upon in the vampire community."

"Oh yeah? What's the big problem, besides the fact that you don't really get a choice in the matter," Beau asked suddenly having his stomach twist up into knots at the mention that Tobias was engaged. Beau wasn't too sure why he felt like he wanted to hurt Tobias's wife to be, but he tried his best to not let his dark emotions reach his face.

"If I were to find my life mate after having been forced into this marriage then the council, who are a group of vampires that we rotate through kind of like your government, would have to have me kill my parents and my then wife," Tobias explained as he managed to look back at Beau. "The life mate takes priority over everything and if there is anything that is trying to get in the way of that it is disposed of."

"Oh," Beau said quietly as he looked down at his hands. *Were life mates really that important to the vampire community?*

"I'm going to try to get out of the marriage because I don't want to be responsible for someone else's death," Tobias commented quietly as he stared directly at Beau.

"Oh? Do you think that you found you life mate?" Beau asked hesitantly as he glanced up at Tobias from underneath his lashes.

"Maybe," Tobias whispered as he continued to stare directly at Beau. Tobias gave his head a quick shake before glancing over to Beau's t-shirt. "Is your shirt dry yet?"

Beau looked over to the t-shirt and sat up on his knees to reach over to the railing and grab it. Beau grimaced as he grabbed the still soaking wet shirt and pulled it off the railing.

"Nope, not even close," Beau replied as he sighed with the still soaked t-shirt in his hands.

"Hmm, alright, well let's head back to my house and you can borrow one of my shirts until yours gets to be dry enough to wear," Tobias said as he stood up from the bench and held out his hand to Beau.

Chapter 20

Beau waited on the marble front porch as Tobias peeked in the front door of his house. Tobias had mentioned that he had gotten into a bit of trouble with his mother when she had found out that there was company at the house that she had not approved of. Beau had asked if it really was okay for him to be coming back to the house again, but Tobias had reassured him that he was fine to be there.

"Alright, it looks like the coast is clear," Tobias called back over his shoulder before widening the door enough for Beau to get in the door too. Beau walked into the front foyer and waited as Tobias shut the door behind them. Tobias led Beau over to the staircase that was at the very end of the foyer, and up the left set of stairs. He led Beau down the hallway that was on the left, passing by many more large dark oak doors.

Everything looked so similar that Beau knew that he would immediately get lost if he didn't have Tobias with him to lead the way. There was nothing distinct about any of the doors that they passed but everything looked spotless, almost like someone obsessively cleaned the entire mansion everyday.

Tobias paused in the hallway and Beau turned his head to look to see if this was his room. But Tobias had his eyes closed and the tips of his ears kept twitching like he was listening for something. Then his eyes popped open and he stared at Beau with wide frightened eyes.

"We need to run," Tobias whispered as he grabbed Beau by the wrist.

"What?" Beau asked not catching what Tobias had said but didn't get an answer as he was whisked off his feet and down the hallway in Tobias's arms. Tobias moved at such a blinding speed that when he finally stopped Beau couldn't stand up straight because he was so dizzy. Tobias quickly opened the door that they were standing in front of and roughly shoved Beau into the room as he glanced nervously down the hallway. Tobias closed the door as quickly and as quietly as he could, before he breathed a sigh of relief leaning his head against the wooden door.

"That was too close," Tobias muttered against the door before he turned around to check on Beau. "Sorry, my father had come home earlier than he usually did and was on the verge of walking up the stairs before I had managed to be able to hear him coming. We should be good now though, I think, but I'll keep an ear out just to be safe."

"Does your father not really like humans?" Beau asked as he brushed himself off and then rubbed at the soreness of his wrist from where Tobias had grabbed him.

"Well, he just sees them as a food source and not much else," Tobias explained as he leaned his back on the door. "I guess he just has lost his respect for humans. He doesn't see them as more than just a food source. I see humans as creatures who have a life of their own just like I do, because of our difference in views my father doesn't really like how I treat the other humans that live here as companions as well as food."

"Oh, I see," Beau said as he fiddled with the wet t-shirt that was in his hands as he looked around the room. It looked like a regular kid's room that he would find nowadays and not 200 years ago. There was a king-sized bed in the middle of the room, which looked like it was way too big for Tobias considering that he was the same smallish size as Beau. There was an oil painting of a sunrise that was coming up over an ocean that sat on the wall opposite of Tobias's bed, but there were no windows in the entire room. There was a small lamp light that had come on by the bed when they had entered the room, and that appeared to be the only light that was in the entire room.

"Well, let's get you something a bit warmer to wear while we wait for your shirt to dry," Tobias said as he walked towards his closet, motioning for Beau to join him. Tobias pulled open his closet doors and flicked on the light that dangled from the ceiling inside the closet. It was no normal run of the mill closet; it was a massive walk-in closet that was so organized that it made Beau not want to touch anything. Why was this entire house so immaculate? It was kind of unnerving to Beau.

Tobias walked towards the back of the closet and swiped through the different t-shirts that were hanging on padded clothes hangers. A lot of the shirts appeared like fancy dress shirts or weird white shirts with white role ties on the front of it or on the sides. At the very end of the rack of shirts there were a few regular graphic t-shirts, some with the graphics were worn off them showing how much they were loved. Tobias flipped between two t-shirts, indecisive about which one he wanted to give Beau to wear.

"I think that this one should be fine for now," Tobias said as he pulled down a black short sleeve t-shirt from the rack. On the t-shirt was a cute little cartoon bat with the words 'I am the Night' written in a curve below the picture of the bat. Beau did his best to disguise his laugh, but the shirt was just too funny to not laugh at, especially with this whole situation. Beau took the shirt from Tobias as he was still trying to stifle his laugh and tried to pull it on over his head. As soon as Beau got the shirt on he felt himself be slammed up against what must've been a wooden cupboard in the closet.

Beau's head throbbed from where it had hit the cupboard but with Tobias now being mere centimetres from his face, Beau barely registered the pain. Tobias was way too close, however, no matter how hard Beau tried he couldn't seem to escape his iron grip or even form any kind of words.

Beau was completely enraptured by Tobias and noticing for the first time the multitude of different colours in Tobias's eyes. The swirling colours in his red eyes were mesmerizing, making Beau's eyelids droop to only being half open.

Beau felt weird, uncomfortable, and hot under Tobias's gaze. He had no idea what was going on with his body and it made him a bit more afraid than usual. Beau vaguely noticed that Tobias's upper fangs had extended past his lower lip, but his brain felt so fuzzy that he wasn't too sure if he was seeing things right; it was almost like he was in a trance or a dream.

Tobias gently grabbed Beau's chin and pulled it slightly to the right, exposing Beau's neck, while Tobias's other hand pulled the neck of Beau's shirt away from the area to allow for a more open access. Tobias leaned in and opened his mouth, preparing to sink his teeth into the soft flesh of Beau's neck. Beau's sweet scent mixed with his own more earthy scent from the t-shirt that Beau was wearing was driving his senses crazy, he wanted to taste Beau's blood.

As Tobias was about to sink his teeth into Beau's neck he started to feel sick, his stomach felt like it was tearing itself apart and his throat felt like it was being burned raw. He quickly snapped his mouth shut, making a clicking noise as his teeth clanged together. Tobias knew that he couldn't do it, even with Beau responding so willingly, without the actual verbal consent Tobias wouldn't be able to drink from Beau. So instead of doing that Tobias stuck his nose in the crook of Beau's neck and breathed in deeply, forcing himself to suffer in the delicious scent of Beau's blood, his forbidden fruit. In this pause Beau was finally able to start to think properly and find his voice again.

"What...what...um...You're not going to...?" Beau murmured as he coughed quietly to clear his throat, not trying to move from his spot since he was still a bit nervous that he might anger Tobias. Tobias let go of Beau's chin as he shook his head slowly, rubbing his cold nose against Beau's neck and shoulder. "W-why?"

Tobias pulled back from Beau and looked him in the eyes. The whites of his eyes had gone black, his eyes looked much more predatory and a lot less human like, with his pupils narrowing like the eyes of a cat. Instead of green cat eyes staring back at him the eyes were red, and darker than usual. Beau swallowed hard but couldn't look away from Tobias's eyes, being sucked back into the mesmerizing colours though predominantly red.

"I can't, not without the permission from the person that I'm drinking from, verbal permission," Tobias replied making sure to clarify the last part. Beau fell out of the trance just long enough to be able to form a cohesive question.

"Is that like the whole thing about asking for entry into people's houses?" Beau asked as he slowly started to come back to his senses. Tobias gave Beau a crooked toothy smile.

"Yeah, something like that," Tobias replied softly as the black began to fade from his eyes.

Chapter 21

"Why does everything in this place feel so brand new?" Beau asked as he hoisted himself up onto Tobias's bed. "I thought that it would've felt older and darker."

"Don't believe all of the stereotypes that you see on the internet," Tobias replied with a smile as he got up on the other side of the bed and sat cross-legged facing Beau. He didn't want to get too close to Beau with what had almost happened in the closet, he was afraid that he was going to make Beau uncomfortable. "We have a good up keep on the house and update the house every five to ten years. We actually just finished putting in a gymnasium on the lower level of the house a few years ago since we've been starting to have to stay in the house more and more often."

Tobias rubbed the back of his neck and smiled sheepishly at Beau as he shifted how he sat on the bed, the blue veins clearly visible on his cheeks and neck.

"Did you maybe want to go down to the gym and learn how to use a sword?" Tobias asked quietly. "I can understand if you'd rather not, with what had just happened and all..."

"Sure! Sounds really cool!" Beau replied as he leaned towards Tobias on the bed, cutting off the rest of what Tobias was going to say. Tobias's mood brightened at Beau's enthusiasm and he managed a relatively natural smile. Tobias was on the other side of the bed standing in front of Beau before Beau even had the chance to blink. He held his hand out to Beau and Beau took it without hesitation.

They walked over to the door and Tobias carefully opened the door, looking up and down the hallway and listening for anything that might signal trouble for them. But Tobias couldn't hear or see anything out of the ordinary. He dragged Beau out of the room and down the hallway to the stairs that led down to the gym. Once they were both inside the gym, Tobias locked the door that they had just come through, and then

143

jumped with extreme speed to all the other doors in the room locking them up as well.

"Alright that should do it, now we shouldn't be interrupted by any unwelcome guests," Tobias commented when he got back to Beau, floating a couple feet above his head, clapping his hands together in a dusting off motion before planting them on his hips and floating down to Beau.

"Our sword collection is over on that wall," Tobias explained as he pointed to the wall that was to Beau's right. "Pick your favourite and I'll show you how to use it."

Beau smiled to Tobias before jogging over to the wall of swords, staring in awe at all the different sizes and kinds of swords that they had. There were long swords, short swords, jeweled swords, plain swords, curved swords, and straight swords all hanging from hooks on the wall going up to about 15-20 feet high. There were so many that Beau wasn't too sure which one he wanted to try to use.

Then one sword caught his attention. It was a bit on the smaller side, but it was still almost longer than Beau's arm. There wasn't anything fancy about the sword, it

144

was just a very simple straight edged sword, but it felt like the sword was calling to Beau.

Beau gently picked up the sword, grabbing it by the hilt with one hand and holding the blade on the palm of his other hand. As soon as Beau picked it up he could feel it pulse with energy in his hands almost like the sword itself was alive.

"That used to be a witch's weapon," Tobias said from behind Beau as Beau admired the sword up close, now noticing the light engravings of symbols in the blade of the sword.

"Wow, really?" Beau asked as he glanced over to Tobias. "It feels really cool, and almost kind of familiar. Is that possible?"

"Hmm, I don't think so, unless of course you were a witch," Tobias replied as he gave Beau a friendly shove, both laughing.

"There's no way I could be a witch, I'm not a girl," Beau commented as the laughing started to calm down.

"That's true," Tobias commented as he grabbed a long thin sword from off the wall. It kind of looked like those swords that you would see in a fencing match. "Now let's go over onto the mats so that I can show you how to properly hold the sword so that you don't wind up accidently hurting yourself."

Tobias showed Beau how to properly hold the sword, how to slash, defend, parry, and most importantly how to attack. Tobias had Beau run through a couple drills with the practise dummies that they had on the other side of the gym.

"You learn pretty fast; did you want to try sparring with me?" Tobias asked as he walked backwards onto the gym mats. "I promise that I won't go too hard on you."

"Alright, but don't go too easy on me either," Beau replied as he walked onto the mats too, giving Tobias a wink before getting into the beginning position that Tobias had showed him. Tobias chuckled before getting into the ready position himself.

"You ready?" Tobias asked as he shifted his weight from his front foot to his back foot.

"Always."

Tobias struck, lunging at Beau with his sword. Beau blocked and pushed Tobias back, making him stumble for a step leaving an opening for Beau to strike. Beau went for a slash, but Tobias recovered quickly and managed to block it. They both exchanged blows, sometimes ducking and rolling to dodge blows from each other. They laughed as they spared, not even really thinking about anything else that could've been going on around them. Then Beau dodged too late on one of Tobias's strikes, the sword cutting into the side of Beau's leg.

"Ow!" Beau said in surprise, quickly reaching down to cover up the cut on his leg from where the sword had grazed him.

"I'm so sorry Beau!" Tobias exclaimed as he rushed over to Beau's side. He helped Beau to limp over to a wooden bench so that Beau could sit down and better inspect the wound.

"It's okay, it doesn't look to be all that bad," Beau commented before sticking his leg out in Tobias's direction. "See?"

As Tobias looked at the wound and the blood he could feel his fangs extend past his lips and his throat go dry with thirst. Tobias barely realized what he was doing in time to be able to stop himself. He threw himself all the way to the other side of the gym with a hand covering his mouth.

"What's wrong?" Beau asked confused as he glance between Tobias and his leg, before managing to connect the dots. "Ohh, are you really that hungry?"

Tobias dropped his eyes and slowly nodded, keeping his hand firmly over his mouth. He knew that he couldn't get any closer or they would both be in trouble.

"Well I don't really know what'll happen if you bite me, but I mean it should be okay for you to just have a taste, right?" Beau asked as he looked down at the cut on his leg, watching as the blood slowly dripped down from the wound. He felt a rush of air coming from Tobias's direction and slowly looked up to look back to Tobias, seeing that he was now directly in front of Beau. The whites of Tobias's eyes had gone black and his fangs were exposed beyond his lower lip.

"You do know what you're saying, right?" Tobias asked Beau, frustrated with Beau's lack of fear or understanding of how dangerous this situation was. "I don't know how this could affect you Beau, because I honestly don't know how my parents and other family members had managed to get their sheep. You could be completely under my control from just this small amount of blood and saliva exchange."

"I'm sure that it'll be fine," Beau replied as he angled his leg to the side so that Tobias could see the wound on his calf more clearly. Tobias stared at the wound hungrily but didn't make a move towards it. "Oh right, I give you permission to drink the blood from my wound."

Tobias practically dropped to his knees in front of Beau and pulled the leg a bit closer to himself. Tobias began to gently and tentatively lick at the blood that had already slipped down Beau's leg. Tobias stopped for a moment and stared at the wound, making a low growling noise in his throat before licking at the wound on Beau's leg. Beau winced in the beginning but as Tobias licked the wound it began to close back up. Tobias sat back on his heels after he had finished, wiping his mouth with the back of his hand.

"I have a bit of an odd question," Beau started blushing a bit as he hesitated, his leg tingling from where the wound used to be.

"What's that?" Tobias asked as he licked his lips and cocked his head to the side.

"What does my blood taste like to you?" Beau asked not being able to meet Tobias's eyes because of how embarrassing the question sounded now that he had said it out loud. Tobias chuckled before he gave the question some thought.

"You taste like...hmmm...this dessert that I used to have when I was still human; I could never get enough of it back then," Tobias replied finally after a few moments of thought. "But I think that you were right. I don't think that that was enough blood for either of us to get too attached to each other, so you should be fine. It's going to be dawn soon though, we should probably go check on your shirt before we start to head back to your house."

Chapter 22

Tobias lowered Beau to the ground less than a block away from the boys' home. Beau's shirt was still wet, so he wound up having to wear Tobias's shirt back to his home, with his wet one slung over his shoulder. When they reached the ground, they were both hesitant to leave, even with the sun on the verge of the horizon.

"Do you want to hang out next Friday as well?" Tobias asked as he floated a couple inches off the ground in front of Beau.

"Of course! I'll try to be on time next time though," Beau replied as he laughed nervously. He wasn't too sure whether Ms. Kay would let him go so easily as she had this time, it had seemed like she had deliberately tried to stop him from going.

"Alright, until next time then,"
Tobias replied with a bow in the air before
he took off back towards his home. With a
smile on his face Beau made the short trek
back to the boys' home, pausing at the door
when he saw the camera on the side of the
house again. The sight of it just seemed to
piss Beau off, even though he knew that it
couldn't possibly be just meant for him.

Beau did his best to quietly sneak
into the front door of the house and tiptoe
into the kitchen. As Beau walked through
the kitchen and passed the study, he could
hear Kyle and Ms. Kay talking in the study.
What were they doing up so late?

They must've thought that he wasn't
home yet because they were talking loud
enough that Beau could hear them. Beau
slowed his pace but chided himself for being
so nosey. He continued through the kitchen
to the stairwell that led to the upper floors.
As Beau stepped up onto the stairs he heard
Ms. Kay and Kyle say something that made
Beau stop dead in his tracks.

"What are we supposed to do about
the thing that has become attached to Beau?"
Kyle asked, he sounded nervous to Beau's
ears.

"I'll make a call and that thing will disappear from Beau's life. I won't allow this one little cretin to mess with the plans for Beau," Beau knew that that was Ms. Kay's voice, but it just didn't sound like her. The voice sounded angry, frustrated, and dark, almost like the bad guy in those video games that he had watched the older boys play. "They must never find out what Beau truly is."

Were they talking about Tobias? But how did they know that Tobias wasn't normal? And what did they know about Beau that even he didn't know about himself. Beau stood on the steps of the stairs, terrified and confused, especially since he had only caught the tail end of their conversation. He snapped out of his trance when he heard a loud noise coming from the study. Not wanting to get caught, he quickly and quietly made his way up the stairs and down the hallway to his room.

Beau leaned his back against the door of his room once he had closed it behind him and tried his best to slow down his racing heart. He knew that they had to be talking about Tobias, but how had they managed to find out about him? He had to figure out a way to warn Tobias, *but about what?* He had no real idea as to what Kyle and Ms. Kay were really talking about in the study. He just knew now that he couldn't trust either of them. It felt like his world was being torn apart from all around him, and the only steadfast thing in his life now was the fact that Tobias was his best friend and that Beau needed to be more careful about what he was saying from now on.

Beau pushed himself to his feet and stumbled over to his bed, stripping down to his underwear as he climbed behind the warm covers. Just as he was about to drift off to sleep his eyes fell on the t-shirt that Tobias had given him. Beau smiled and reached down to grab the t-shirt, tucking it under his pillow so that no one would find it in the morning. That shirt was the one thing that Beau was not willing to share with anyone especially the other boys.

Beau snuggled back into the blankets and rested his head on the pillow, slowly drifting off into a deep sleep.

Chapter 23

Monday morning Beau went off to school early to make sure that he didn't have to talk to anyone, making sure not to act unusual to Kyle or Ms. Kay but also to not share anything that wasn't necessary. They had asked him a couple things when he had woken up late on Saturday morning, but Beau did his best to skirt around the questions saying that he was too tired to talk about it. Ms. Kay didn't bother to ask any more questions after that morning, but Kyle did. He seemed worried and nervous as he asked the questions. But that wasn't what had freaked Beau out that had made him leave the house to go to school Monday morning without talking to anyone.

As Beau walked to the school in the crisp morning air, he thought back on that weird conversation that he had had with Kyle literally the night before. Kyle had come up to his room with a book hidden underneath of his shirt. He had closed the door and locked it behind him before turning to look at Beau. He had said something about not being able to do what Ms. Kay had asked him to do anymore and that Beau deserved to know the truth.

Then he had pulled the book out and tossed it to Beau, if he really wanted to know the truth and if his friend was really a creature of the night then he would want to read this. Kyle had said that he had thought that they were just protecting him, meaning Ms. Kay and himself, but he knew better now and wanted Beau to be able to protect himself. Then he had left, with just a warning over his shoulder that he should never let the book out of his sight.

The book that Kyle had tossed at Beau was now shoved deep into his backpack. It was a black leather-bound book with strings around the book to keep it closed, the pages inside the book had gone slightly yellow, and it looked like it had been handwritten with black ink. He hadn't bothered to read what was inside the book last night, just glanced at it before hiding the book away under the far corner of his mattress. Kyle hadn't bothered to approach him again after that, in fact it kind of seemed like Kyle was starting to avoid him again.

Beau tried to push these thoughts out of his mind as he finally made it to the front of the school yard. Since Beau had met Tobias he has been in a more cheerful mood at school and people seem to be taking more of a liking to him now. Being less of an outcast at the school has forced the bullies to back down now knowing that Beau had people watching his back. In fact, one of his new friends had just arrived at the school as well and waved to Beau as she came up the sidewalk. Her name was Kiki and she liked to play basketball as well as floor hockey, and she had a very feisty attitude that could make her very scary if it was turned on you.

"Hey Beau!" Kiki said as she started walking right next to Beau as they walked up to the front doors of the school together. They chatted about their weekend and Kiki mentioned about this tournament that she had coming up for basketball and was wondering if Beau had wanted to come and watch. Beau said that he would if it wasn't on Friday night or Saturday since he already had other plans.

"That's fine I think that it's on the Thursday of this week anyway," Kiki replied as she tapped her fingers on her desk in thought. Both Beau and Kiki were sitting at their desks in the classroom as they waited for their teacher to come in to start the classes.

"Alright, would you mind picking me up? I don't think that Ms. Kay would want to drive me anywhere," Beau asked as he leaned on the back of his chair so that he could talk to Kiki who was sitting directly behind him.

"Sure! That way you can't chicken out," Kiki said as she laughed giving Beau a playful poke in the chest. Beau rubbed at the spot where Kiki had poked at him but smiled ruefully at her as he did so. They chatted for a bit longer until the rest of the students and the teacher arrived for the class to start.

When school ended Kiki and Beau chatted together as they left the building, saying goodbye at the front of the school as they had to go their separate ways to get to their homes. On the way back home, Beau had this sudden feeling of dread clench in the pit of his stomach and a massive headache just spring out of nowhere.

He figured he'd take a detour home and maybe spend some time alone at the park for a bit before heading back to the house. The dread in his stomach lessened a bit as he changed directions and headed towards the park, but the headache just wouldn't go away, and the aching spread to his neck and shoulders.

When Beau got to the park there were a couple other kids there playing on the jungle gym, but the swings were still free. Beau took a seat on one of the swings, dropping his backpack on the ground in front of him, and reaching in and pulling out the old, black leather book that Kyle had given him. As Beau gently rocked on the swing he began to slowly flip through the worn and yellowed pages, the only thing that was on the pages were weird symbols that didn't appear to be in any kind of normal language.

The more pages that Beau flipped through and concentrated on, the more the symbols started to become familiar and seem to shift into letters and then words. But there was nothing that he could read that was concrete or made any kind of sense. Some of the symbols didn't change and remained just symbols no matter how hard Beau concentrated on them.

After a while Beau knew that he was going to have to leave the park and head home since he hadn't told Ms. Kay that he was going to be going to the park after school. He packed up his backpack and threw it over his shoulder as he started off for the boys' home. Beau knew that he was going to get an earful if he didn't get to the house soon.

Chapter 24

Beau scrubbed the last of the dishes from dinner, his hands wrinkled from being in the water, so long. Ms. Kay had been very mad at Beau when had gotten back to the house and had decided to punish him with cleaning all the dishes and the entire kitchen all by himself. By the time that Beau had finished cleaning up everything in the kitchen it was nearly 8:30 at night. Beau dried off his hands before rubbing at the sides of his head, the headache was still there. He had mentioned it to Ms. Kay, but she had just brushed him off, probably thinking that he was trying to get out of his punishment.

Beau held his hand over his scarred eye as he felt the headache spread to the front of his head. Thinking that maybe some sleep would help, Beau went over to the study and told Ms. Kay that he was going to go to bed early tonight. She looked to Beau with a small smile and nodded, not saying anything since she was busy discussing something with someone over the phone. It seemed like it was becoming a heated conversation, so Beau thought that it was best not to say anything more to her for the moment. Though he did have some questions about the black leather book, Kyle had said that he shouldn't mention the book to anyone else.

Beau left the kitchen and went up the stairs to his bedroom. He slipped into some pajamas and tucked himself into bed, checking to make sure that the book was still tucked underneath the corner of the mattress before settling in to try to get some sleep. Listening to the sounds of the other boys playing video games as he slowly drifted off into sleep, with the headache still throbbing.

Beau was awoken in the middle of the night by a quiet but insistent knocking coming from the window. He groggily got out of his bed and stumbled over to the window, the headache still pounding in the front of his head making it difficult for Beau to keep his balance.

Beau immediately woke up when he saw that Tobias was hovering just outside the window. Beau threw open the window and let Tobias in to the room. Tobias floated into the room and gingerly sat down on the top of Beau's desk, wincing as he did so. As Tobias got closer to Beau he was finally able to get a good look at Tobias.

Tobias had blisters climbing up his neck and arms, and a couple bruises on his face and wrists. There were also a couple burn marks on the upper part of his chest that went below his shirt, but there was something missing.

"What happened? Where's your jacket?" Beau asked in a hushed voice as he stood right in front of Tobias, lifting his chin a bit to get a better look at the wounds that were on Tobias's face.

"Silver mostly, but someone had tipped off my parents that I was hanging out with you," Tobias replied as he winced trying to smile. "My arguing didn't help the situation though either. They destroyed my jacket as part of my punishment, as well as doing a few other things, but that's not why I came here."

Tobias sighed and closed his eyes for a moment, memorizing the feeling of Beau's hands on his face.

"I made a deal with them that I would take my punishment without a fight if they were to leave you alone. But they said that the only way that they would leave you alone was if I married my fiancée and if I never saw you again," Tobias said as he opened his eyes so that Beau could see that even his predatory side didn't want this.

Beau wasn't sure what he should say or do; he didn't want to stop being friends with Tobias, but he didn't want Tobias to be hurt anymore by his family either. Beau watched as black tears spilled from Tobias's eyes, the whites of his eyes long gone and replaced by black. Beau couldn't help the tears that were welling up in his own eyes.

"I don't want you to go, but I don't want to see you getting hurt," Beau replied as tears started to stream down his cheeks as well.

"I'm so sorry," Tobias cried through his tears as he gently grasped Beau's wrists with shaking hands. "But if they ever break their promise I will come and find you no matter where you are, I promise."

Tobias gave Beau a quick kiss on the forehead, lingering for a moment before he took off out the window, closing the window shut behind him as he left. Beau stood staring at the closed window for a moment completely stunned, before it all came crashing down on him.

Beau collapsed onto the floor in front of his desk, sobbing uncontrollably. He felt like his heart was being torn apart and there was nothing that he could do to stop the pain. Once Beau had managed to calm himself down enough, he climbed back into his bed and cried himself to sleep.

When the sun peeked in the window of Beau's room the following morning and the rowdy loud boys had woken up, Beau stayed curled up under the covers as he sniffled softly to himself. He was alone again. The pain from the night before had managed to dull to an ache but it had not stopped, even after Beau had fallen asleep. He could already tell that today was not going to be a good day.

Chapter 25

Beau slumped his way down the stairs and sat at the table with the rest of the boys but didn't touch his food, he didn't feel like eating. Beau sipped at his orange juice and munched on a piece of toast before leaving the table to go back up to his room. He plopped down onto the bed and just stared at the floor, not wanting to get dressed or go to school. He didn't want to stay at the house either though considering that someone in this house had to have been the cause for Tobias's parents finding out, since no one else at Tobias's house had seen them.

...The phone call last night...could that have been to Tobias's parents' house? It couldn't have been, could it? If it was, why would Ms. Kay have their phone number in the first place? Could it have something to do with the black book that Beau was now in possession of? Maybe not, but there might be some answers in the book. Beau knew that he couldn't read the book here since there were too many eyes on him. He had to go to the school and try to read it while he was there.

Beau forced himself to get up from the bed and get dressed for school. He packed the black book into his backpack that he had brought upstairs last night and headed down the stairs to leave for school. Hoping that no one would try to stop him on the way out the front door, or on the way down the sidewalk. He wasn't too sure what he would say to them if they had managed to stop him.

When Beau arrived at the school, he picked a spot in the front yard with some shade and retrieved the book from his bag. He began to flip through the various pages of symbols, stopping near the end of the book when there were actual English words written on the pages. It wasn't Ms. Kay's handwriting or anyone else he knew that had lived in that house, but it was very fancy and seemed feminine in nature.

My Dearest Beau,

I'm sorry that I won't be able to be with you long enough to give you this in person, my son, but I'm sure that my younger sister will help explain some of what's in this book to you.

He stared at those first few words for a moment completely stunned that someone had meant for this book to come to him. He had thought that he had just came from a home that had thrown him out with the morning trash. At least that's the way that Ms. Kay had told the story. But who was this younger sister that the author of this note was speaking of, and why hadn't she found Beau yet? He continued reading the note.

You need to know that you are not any kind of ordinary young boy. You have some very special blood and you can create wonders and protect those around you with the spells that are in this book. But you can also create great pain and destruction if you use the spells for the wrong reasons.

You will be very special to this world, and not just because of how you look. My darling you will be the next…

The last couple pages were torn out of the book, and in their place was an older looking polaroid photo of two young women. One of them was wearing a graduation gown and the other was smiling with their arm around the person in the graduation outfit. The one in the graduation gown looked oddly familiar to Beau but he couldn't seem to place her. He flipped the photo over and read the scribbled marker on the back.

My little sister's graduation June 18, 1995

The little sister looked a lot like a younger version of Ms. Kay. But that couldn't possibly be right could it? Why would she have hidden something so important from him about himself if she was really his aunt that was supposed to be teaching him and taking care of him? This note in the book had left him with more questions than answers. Maybe if he practised some of the more basic spells and stuff that was at the beginning of the book; things might become a little clearer after that.

"Hey Beau!" Beau heard Kiki call his name. He quickly put the book away in his backpack before looking around to see where Kiki was calling to him from. He saw her waving at him from the sidewalk that led up to the school doors. Beau waved back before getting up and jogging over to join her on the sidewalk.

Chapter 26

Beau never told Kiki about the book, in fact, he left the book in his bag for the entire school day. This wasn't something that he could just read at school, especially with him being so exposed like that. If he wanted to read the book he would have to do it in a secluded closed off area without anyone else present. Maybe he could try to do it in the attic of the boys' home, no one ever went up there.

Beau tried to pay attention to Kiki as she waved goodbye to him as they separated at the front of the school, but his mind was elsewhere. He wanted to really know if he was as different as the note has led him to believe, and why he hadn't been told about his other abnormality.

Beau was deep in thought on the way back home that it took him a moment to realize that he was being watched. The hairs on the back of his neck were tingling making him stop walking and shiver. Beau looked around but the only thing that was on the street and anywhere around him was a small dark blue car that was parked some ways back on the other side of the street. The car looked empty as Beau squinted at it to try to get a clearer view of the driver and passenger seats.

Beau shook his head and continued on his way to the boys' home thinking that he had imagined the feeling of being watched, maybe even a little hopeful. His heart ached as he thought back to what Tobias had said before leaving him, and Beau steeled his resolve to learn what was in the book so that he could become stronger and maybe be able to protect Tobias so that his family couldn't hurt him, so that Tobias could be free to make his own choices.

Upon entering the house Beau was relieved to see that there was no one else in sight. He quickly made his way up the stairs and snuck passed the other boys that were preoccupied in the living room. He opened the door that was at the end of the hallway that showed a dark and dusty set of stairs leading up towards the attic.

Beau chanced a glance behind himself but didn't see anyone else in the hallway behind him. He felt around on the walls of the stairway until he felt something that seemed like a grimy light switch. He flicked the switch and sighed in relief when the light slowly flickered on. Beau slowly and quietly closed the door behind himself making sure that it clicked shut before he cautiously made his way up the creaky wooden steps. He peered over the edge of the stairs to the floor of the attic, seeing only boxes stacked up against the walls.

Beau climbed up the remaining steps and walked across the attic floor, stopping in the centre of the floor. He knelt and slid the backpack off his back, unzipping the bag and pulling out the black leather book. Beau sat cross legged on the floor and flipped the book open to the first page. Reading the first few steps about how to develop the ability to call forth and focus the power that is within.

The first thing that Beau had to do was find some chalk so that he could draw a circle on the floor with a pentagram inside of it. He got up and went over to the first set of boxes and began shifting through the stuff in the dusty boxes. There had to be something up in the attic that he could use to draw the symbol on the floor. After going

173

through roughly ten different boxes Beau was finally able to find a box with a bunch of old summer supplies that had been long forgotten, and in that box was some old sidewalk chalk.

"Yes!" Beau whispered to himself as he grabbed a hold of the small box of thick pieces of sidewalk chalk. He fingered through the pieces of chalk trying to find a white piece but settled for a smaller yellow piece of chalk. Beau walked back over to the centre of the floor and drew a large circle first before drawing a large pentagram in the middle that would be big enough for Beau to be able to sit in, and whose five points touched five different parts of the circle.

Beau went back to the book after drawing the symbol on the floor. He read through the next couple steps which stated that to do the procedure properly he had to sit in a Full Lotus position. At first, he was confused by the term "Full Lotus" but in the brackets that came after the term it explained that it was a cross legged position in which the bottoms of the feet are facing the ceiling rather than the floor. Then breathe deeply as he focused on clearing his mind with his hands resting on his knees.

Beau nodded slowly to himself as he finished reading the steps thinking that this seemed easy enough to be able to do. He put the book down just outside the circle and walked into the middle of the pentagram, sitting down in the pentagon that had been created through the drawing of the pentagram. He got into the Full Lotus position with some difficulty, making a mental note to start stretching more, and rested his hands on his knees. Beau closed his eyes taking slow deep breaths as he tried his best to clear his mind and just feel what was within him and around him.

After a few moments where nothing seemed to happen Beau became frustrated and opened his eyes so that he could get up. When Beau opened his eyes and saw what he was doing his mouth dropped open, seconds before his butt hit the floor. He groaned and rubbed his butt as his brain slowly caught up with what he had just seen. He had been levitating at least a good foot or foot and a half off the ground before he had lost his concentration.

Beau stared at his hands in a daze for a moment, his hands were shaking badly and didn't seem to be any close to stopping. He stuck his hands underneath his armpits to try to get them to calm down as he started to nervously laugh to himself. He just couldn't believe it. Everything that he had been told to by Ms. Kay was a lie. He hadn't been thrown away like he had always been thought, and he wasn't a weaker child like he had always been told that he was because of his Albinism.

But the one thing that had really struck him the hardest, besides the fact that the one person that he had trusted most had lied to him, was the fact that he really was a male witch.

Chapter 27

When Beau had heard Ms. Kay call to come down stairs and eat dinner he had already returned to his room from the attic and was laying on his bed while staring up at the bottom of the top bunk, thinking heavily. He slowly sat up and headed towards the stairs that led down to the kitchen. He paused at the top of the stairs as he thought about how he was going to react with everything that he had just found out. How was he supposed to act normal? He had to ask Ms. Kay what was really going on. It would probably be safest to do it in front of the other boys since she couldn't do anything to him with all of them there.

Beau slowly descended the stairs and kept his head down as he took an empty seat at the table. His fingers kept fidgeting with a string that was coming off the one side of his pants. He wasn't sure if he really wanted to go through with his plan of asking the lady of the house his questions, but he did need to get some answers, and this seemed like the only way that he was going to be able to get them.

As Beau took a few bites of his food, he mulled around in his mind how he was going to be able to ask what he wanted to ask without making the lady of the house mad at him. He glanced down to the end of the table where Ms. Kay sat eating her dinner through the chaos of the other boys talking loudly and eating rather messily. Maybe he should just ask if she had an older sister, that seemed like the safest question to ask.

"Umm, Ms. Kay, can I ask you a question?" Beau asked hesitantly as he put down his eating utensils and mustered up his courage.

"Of course," Ms. Kay replied as she set down her own utensils, the other boys that were sitting at the table had quieted down a bit after hearing Ms. Kay speak.

"W-were you like us?" Beau asked as he tried to keep himself calm and innocent in appearance.

"What do you mean?"

"I-I mean did you ever have any other family, like siblings?"

Ms. Kay was silent for a moment, just looking at Beau. It seemed like she was contemplating as to why he would be asking this all of the sudden, but he couldn't be sure that that was what she was really thinking. Ms. Kay smiled but there seemed to be something off about it. It looked different than usual to Beau at least, no one else seemed to notice. Except out of the corner of his eye he could see Kyle swallow hard and keep his eyes focused on his plate.

"Hmm, I think that I used to have some family, but you know what the funny thing is? Your family always winds up betraying you in one way or another in the end," Ms. Kay replied with a giggle, she appeared to be trying to make light on what she had just said. After hearing that though, Beau was now more alert than he ever was and more afraid. He knew better now more than ever that he shouldn't ask her any more of his questions. He'd have to find a different way to get the answers that he so desperately wanted.

"Was that all that you wanted to ask?" Ms. Kay asked as she picked up her fork and stabbed at a piece of broccoli with the smile still on her face.

"Y-yes," Beau stuttered out as he quickly went back to eating his dinner, making sure to keep his eyes focused on his plate. There was now no one left that he could turn to, and he sure didn't want to involve Kiki in all this mess that he had gotten himself into. Tobias may have helped him if he could've but that was no longer possible. If only he knew how much stronger Beau was getting, then maybe things wouldn't have gone so wrong.

Chapter 28

"So, your tournament is tomorrow night, right?" Beau asked as he walked with Kiki down the hallway of the school towards their first period class.

"Yep! You're still coming right?" Kiki asked as she stopped Beau in the hallway with a worried expression on her face. Beau chuckled and continued walking as he called back to her over his shoulder.

"The only thing that could keep me away is if I was kidnapped," Beau joked as he heard Kiki run up behind him to catch up. She kept pace beside him and gave him a playful shove with her elbow.

"You better not get kidnapped then," Kiki growled as she smiled at Beau just before she messed up his hair with her hand and took off into the classroom. Beau groaned and tried to fix his hair with his hand before realizing that it was hopeless and walked into the classroom too. He had never been to a girl's basketball tournament before and was looking forward to being able to go to the event with her. It would probably be the first event that another human has invited him out to in nearly six years.

The day felt so relaxed and normal that Beau had nearly forgotten about Tobias, about his aunt, Ms. Kay, lying to him, and about the little secret that he was now hiding about himself. He felt like everything was going to be alright for those few hours, well, until he slipped up that was.

"Hey! What are you drawing in your workbook?" Kiki asked as she turned around in her chair to face Beau. Beau looked at her for a second, confused as to what she was talking about, before looking down at his workbook. His eyes went wide as he saw that he had unconsciously began drawing the symbols that he had seen in the black leather book that his mother had given him.

"Umm, its nothing I'm just doodling," Beau replied and quickly closed his workbook so that Kiki wouldn't be able to get a closer look at the symbols that he had draw repeatedly all over the page.

"Well, can I see them?" Kiki asked as she reached for Beau's workbook. "They looked really pretty and interesting."

"Umm, no I'm sorry but you can't it's a bit personal," Beau replied trying to avoid the question without completely avoiding Kiki's gaze.

"But I thought that you had just said that you were just doodling?"

"I was, but it was about something personal that I don't really want to show you right now."

Kiki pouted at Beau but withdrew her hand and turned back around in her seat as the teacher began speaking to the class. Beau relaxed his shoulders as he felt like he was mostly out of the woods with Kiki asking questions about his doodles. She might ask a couple more things, but he would be more prepared when she did since he would've had more time to think of some responses in advance.

Beau couldn't let another leak like that happen again. He was just lucky that he hadn't done that at the boys' home, that would've been much more troublesome trying to explain that away. He needed more practise at keeping his powers and thoughts under control so that he wouldn't have another incident. He made a mental note to go up to the attic and try to do some more meditating before dinner.

Beau was relieved when Kiki didn't ask about the doodles again, and they separated with Beau feeling both relaxed and determined. He made the walk back to the boys' home and said a quick hello to the boys that were in the kitchen before heading up the stairs. He dropped his backpack off in his room and proceeded to head towards the door that led to the attic.

Once safely alone in the attic, Beau went straight for the box of summer supplies. He pulled out the yellow piece of chalk and the black leather book that he had left up there from the last time he had a chance to meditate. He drew the penacle on the floor and got into the cross-legged position in the middle. He brought the black book in with him and placed the book just in front of him.

Beau relaxed and cleared his mind, breathing deeply as he focused on his surroundings. He opened his eyes and saw the black leather book was floating in front of him at eye level. The book flipped open to the page of spells that Beau had left off at learning how to use and stayed there as Beau carefully read through the spell as he floated over a foot off the ground.

Chapter 29

"Beau! There are some people here who want to meet you," Beau barely heard Ms. Kay call to him from down two flights of stairs. Beau groaned and dropped his feet down from his levitated position of his meditation circle.

"I'll be down in a minute!" Beau called back as he walked over to the summer supplies box where he pulled out a cloth and wiped the chalk lines off the floor. He brought the book down the first flight of stairs with him to his room and hid the black leather book back under the corner of his mattress. Beau threw the cloth into the laundry hamper that was in the bathroom on the way down the hallway to the stairs that led to the kitchen.

Beau made his way down the stairs but slowed his pace when he saw that there was a younger looking woman and a young man sitting across the table from Ms. Kay. Beau stopped on the last step of the stairs and glanced between them with his eyebrows scrunched up together.

"What's going on?" Beau asked quietly as he remained rooted on the last step of the stairs, not wanting to take that last step into the kitchen, fearing what could've been taking place that they would need to have him present for.

"Beau come over here and sit down, we have something that we want to talk to you about," Ms. Kay said as she gestured to the open seat that was next to her. Beau hesitated with his hand still holding tight to the railing. The couple looked like a young married couple and the only viable reason that Beau could think of that they would be here was if they were looking at adopting.

Beau swallowed and let go of the railing, stepping down the last step of the stairs. He shuffled over to the table with his hands at his sides and his back straight. He kept a straight face as he took the chair that was next to Ms. Kay. She was smiling and tried to encourage Beau to smile but he just kept up the solemn face, he knew what she was trying to do. Any other time he probably would've been happy for an opportunity like this, to finally have a family. But Beau knew that there was no way that this was just by chance that they had shown up a couple days after Beau had asked about Ms. Kay's life.

"He's just as cute as his pictures!" the young woman said excitedly as she looked to her partner, clinging onto his upper arm. He chuckled at her enthusiasm and patted her hand that was gripping his arm. Beau tried not to react to the compliment and just simply nodded his acknowledgement to the lady. "He's definitely the one that we've been looking for, isn't he sweetie?"

"Most definitely," the man said as he stared directly at Beau. They seemed normal enough at first glance to Beau. Maybe it was just a regular family that he was being sent off to. He figured that it might be better than being stuck in this claustrophobic house. The only thought that comforted Beau with the idea of moving out of the house was what Tobias had said about always being able to find him when he needed to. Beau just hoped that he was right about that.

The couple talked about the house that Beau would be staying in and saying that he would have his own room and a huge yard to play in, since they owned several acres of land out in the country. It seemed like a nice idea to finally have a chance at a home after having lost everything that he had ever cared about. But the only issue was was that he wasn't allowed to tell his friends that he was moving away since there wasn't any time to do so. The couple wanted Beau to move into their house that very day if he wanted to give them a chance at being a family.

Beau sat quietly at the table as the couple looked at Beau expectantly. He could see Ms. Kay smile out of corner of his eye. She really did want him out of the house, badly. Well it couldn't be all that bad living in the country, and he would finally get his own personal space to sleep.

"Okay," Beau replied quietly as he played with his fingers in his lap. The couple looked very excited and happy that he wanted to go with them, but all of this seemed kind of rushed. Didn't they need to fill out paperwork or something to make this official?

"Alright, well, go up and pack a bag of the stuff that you want to take with you and say your goodbyes to the other boys," Ms. Kay said as she clasped her hands together. "We'll finish up all the paperwork down here, and you should be able to leave by the time you get back down here."

Beau nodded slowly and excused himself from the table, trying not to make it look like he was rushing up the stairs. His stomach was full of tight knots the entire time he was walking up the steps. The nerves constricted his throat the moment that he saw Kyle standing at the top of the stairs with a black eye.

"I'm sorry," was all that he whispered as his eyes filled with tears, he turned away and slumped back down the hallway to his room without another word to Beau, locking the door behind him as he closed the door. Suddenly, Beau was regretting the decision that he had just made becoming very alert to all the sounds around him. He just hoped that he was wrong about the bad feeling that he was getting from what Kyle had just said.

Chapter 30

"Here we are!" Beau's new mother said as she pushed open the door to the smallish looking farm house. Once she opened the door, the house didn't appear all that small at all on the inside. When they had first pulled up to the house all Beau was able to see was a treeline that was thick enough that he couldn't see anything that was beyond the trees. Beau didn't even see the entrance to the driveway until they had already pulled onto it.

There were trees all around the front of the house and a small garden that was under the front window of the house that was next to the front door. It was just a single level house but it looked cute and homely from the outside so that was a nice start. Once he was inside the home and being ushered into the living room by his new mother.

It was a lot bigger than Beau had thought that it would be, but it was also a lot emptier than he had thought that it would be. There was no pictures or paintings on the walls, or on any of the shelves that Beau had seen as he looked around the room. There was barely any furniture, so Beau figured that they must've been just moving in even though there weren't any cardboard moving boxes that he could see.

"This is the living room and the kitchen, we'll be eating dinner shortly because we know that you haven't eaten yet, but first let us show you to your new room," Beau's new mother said as she started walking towards a doorway that led off the kitchen. Beau followed slowly behind, wondering why they hadn't told him their names and just asked him to call them by the parental terms of "mother" and "father". *Was this how a new home was supposed to be like?*

Beau's new mother stopped in front of a wooden door with a brass doorknob. She pulled a key out from her pocket and unlocked the door before gesturing for Beau to go inside and look around. Beau wasn't sure what he was expecting but it sure wasn't what he saw on the other side of the door. All there was a twin sized cot in front of him and a small desk that was off to the right; there wasn't even a dresser, a closet, or a lamp in the room. This is what Beau imagined that prison must look like.

He tried not to seem ungrateful for allowing him to come into their home and tried for his best smile to his new mother to show his appreciation. It didn't seem like she was paying him much attention though as her cellphone had started ringing. She pulled it out of her back pocket and looked to see who was calling her.

"Dinner will be ready in about 30 minutes, just get comfy and we'll come and get you in a bit," his new mother said before she answered the phone and closed the door behind herself and his father. Beau's nerves went up a notch when he heard the lock click into place. He held tightly onto the straps of his bag as he slowly creeped back towards the bed. This place didn't feel like any kind of home that he would ever want to be a part of, it just felt cold and empty. Maybe after dinner he would tell them that he didn't feel comfortable and that maybe this wasn't such a good idea.

That thought put Beau's mind a bit more at ease, and he sat back on the bed so that he could go through his bag of belongings. He brought out the black book and ran his fingers over the front cover in thought. He couldn't really go back to the boys' home either though, he knew that things would become more strained the longer that he stayed. He supposed that he could run away after they dropped him off at the boys' home, but what if they didn't want to give him back?

Beau's hand froze on the edge of the cover as he glanced around the room. There wasn't even a window in the room, just the door that he had came through. One way in and only one way out. He shook his head to himself as his grip tightened on the leather book in his hands. He was sure that they would understand and see reason in what he was saying and let him go back.

Beau tried his best to distract himself and pass the time by reading through the remaining few symbols that he had yet to memorize. These last few symbols were very complex in design and in what they did when used properly. There was one spell that was on the second to last page that had piqued Beau's interest the most. It was a spell about how to heal otherworldly beings, which apparently needed higher magic doses than that of a regular human or animal. He smiled as he memorizes the symbol and how to perform the spell.

Beau was interrupted by the sound of rapid footsteps coming down the hallway towards his door. He was about to shove his book into the backpack when he felt it shrink to the size of a small notebook. He chuckled and without a second thought shoved it into his front pocket just as the door to his room was unlocked and his "father" stepped into the room, without knocking or otherwise making his presence known. He smiled at Beau as he opened the door.

"Dinner's ready," his father said as he stepped backwards into the hallway and started walking down the hallway back towards the kitchen. Beau got up from the bed and slowly followed, something just didn't feel right. When Beau arrived in the kitchen, dinner was set up at the polished stone square island that stood in the middle of the kitchen. Beau pulled himself up onto one of the stools and waited patiently as his new mother got him some food and set the plate down in front of him. The smell of the delicious pasta made Beau's stomach twist up in hunger.

"Thank you," Beau said quietly as he looked towards his new parents before taking a couple bites of his dinner. After the first few bites Beau wondered why they weren't eating with him. Had they already eaten before coming to get him? That's when it finally started to hit Beau.

It started with a mild headache and then went to dizziness. Beau felt like his head was foggy and he could feel his body start to fall towards the floor, but he couldn't do anything to stop himself from hitting the floor. He could barely keep his eyes open as he glanced around to his parents who had come around the kitchen island. He tried to say or do something, but his body wouldn't respond. He watched with blurred vision as they laughed, before feeling the father grab him by the wrists and drag him across the floor.

Beau blacked out just as he saw them dragging him towards an open doorway that led to what appeared to be a dark stairwell.

Chapter 31

Beau's head pounded like it was being drilled into by a mini-jackhammer. His arms, legs, and lower back throbbed painfully as well. His vision was still blurry and where ever he was it was far too dark for him to be able to see anything too clearly. What had they put in that pasta?

Beau tried to bring his hands up to his head, but his arms felt strangely heavy. He let his eyes slowly adjust to the dark as he managed to move his head around to look down at his wrists. Big, thick, silver looking manacles were around Beau's wrists and attached to the back wall behind him with thick dark chains. Beau's heart began to race at the sight as panic began to sink in.

What had happened to his adoptive parents, and how had he wound up in this dungeon looking place?

The more that Beau's eyes adjusted to the dark and the waning dizziness the faster that Beau's heart raced. The place really did look like a medieval dungeon. Beau flinched backwards when the door, that he didn't notice, on the far side of the room slammed open.

"Mom? Dad?" Beau questioned, hoping that his adoptive parents didn't really do this to him and that they were here to rescue him. It was his adoptive parents that walked through the door, but Beau's heart sank when he realized that it didn't look like they had come down those stairs, that he could see behind them, to rescue him. In fact, Beau thought that they were the ones that had locked him down here in the first place, especially considering how they were dressed. They looked like they were from a gang of some sort with the amount of heavy leather that they were wearing.

"Just tell us about the vampires, kid, and things will go nice and easy for you," the man who had been Beau's adoptive father said as he sneered down at where Beau lay in a heap on the dirt covered ground.

It suddenly clicked to Beau as to who these people really were and why they had wanted him so badly. They were vampire hunters, and they were after Tobias and his family. No matter what happened to him, Beau knew that he couldn't betray Tobias like that. Beau tried his best to act confused from his oddly angled position on the floor, but it didn't seem to even phase them.

"Fine, more fun for us," the woman who used to be his adoptive mother and the person who had drugged him commented with a laugh. She gave a nod to the man and he smiled as they both advanced on Beau who coward under their menacing gazes.

Chapter 32

Beau wasn't too sure how long they were beating him before they decided that they needed to take a coffee break. All Beau knew was that he couldn't move his right arm or his left leg, and he had felt something crack in his chest that was now making it difficult for him to be able to breathe as he laid on his back on the floor. His throat was sore and raw both from screaming and from them grabbing him.

All this pain was beginning to make Beau reconsider why he was even keeping quiet in the first place. Tobias had just left him after all so why did he even need to bother protecting the vampire that had abandoned him. But he knew that he couldn't do that. In Beau's heart he knew that Tobias was not just any ordinary vampire to him, and with that thought Beau knew that he would protect Tobias to his final breath if that's what it was going to take. Just on cue the door on the far side of the room slammed open again. This time Beau didn't even flinch, resolute in his decision.

"Well if he does die we could always sell his body to the Black Market, Albinos always go for more money than regular bodies," the man said to the woman as they walked into the room and towards Beau who lay motionless on the floor.

"Is he already dead?" the woman asked as she poked Beau hard in the ribs with her boot. Beau groaned and hissed at the pain that burned across his body. "Huh, guess not."

"Well, what do you want to do now? I'm out of ideas," the woman commented as she turned to look at the man that was standing beside her.

"Well, the Black Market doesn't mind if they don't get the bodies all in one piece," the man said as he glanced to his partner with an evil smirk on his face.

"Well that's true," the woman agreed as she walked over to a big wooden table that was off to the far-left side of the room. Beau watched with a morbid curiosity as she pulled on a pair of black latex gloves and put a mask over her mouth and nose. Beau didn't start to panic until he saw her pick up a hacksaw that was splattered with red and what looked like black blood.

Beau tried to shuffle away since they had taken the chains off him while they were beating him but screamed when the man's heel came down hard on his ankle with an audible crack. Tears sprang to Beau's eyes both out of fear and the fresh pain that was radiating up his leg from his ankle.

Then the few lights that there were in this basement dungeon went out, and for a second everything was dark. Then the backup lights kicked in and the room was bathed in an eerie red light with a quiet siren wailing in the background, it must've been coming from somewhere above them.

"Stay here with the brat, I'll be right back," the man said as he pulled a pistol out from the back waistband of his pants. Beau watched him leave the room and head up the stairs, pausing only for a moment to close the door behind him.

The lady put the saw back down onto the table and pulled out her own pistol from the back of her pants as she eyed the closed door warily. Beau tried his best to keep her in his sights as she moved past a cage and some hanging chains towards the wall where he vaguely remembered there were levers hooked into the wall.

Beau whipped his head back to the door when he heard a set of muffled gunshots ring out in the silence that had befallen them, then a man's screams, and then silence again. Beau's whole body started to shake as he watched the door with wide eyes, terrified and oddly a bit hopeful, knowing full well that the person who could walk through that door next could be an ally just as much as it could just be another enemy.

The basement door slowly creaked open but there was no one in the doorway or even on the stairs, just a small river of blood slowly dripping down the steps. Beau's heart pounded in his ears as he stared at the blood that was dripping down the stairs waiting to see what else was going to follow it, but nothing else came down the stairs. Beau whipped his head over to the woman when he heard her pull one of the heavy levers. He just didn't understand why she would do that, especially when there was no one there.

Beau heard a whistling sound as something small whizzed over his head, and then the whistling started coming from various points of the room all at the same time. A few of what looked like mini arrows stuck in midair and began to leak a black liquid onto the ground. A smoky figure began to appear, slowly solidifying a few feet away from Beau.

"No…" Beau whispered in a pained voice as he stared with wide eyes up at none other than Tobias, his would be rescuer. Tears welled up in Beau's eyes as he took in Tobias's ragged appearance. The mini arrows stuck out of his chest, abdomen, arms, neck and legs, but Tobias was just smiling down at him even with his demonic vampire eyes out in full view.

"...I...found...you..." was all that Tobias could manage before he collapsed onto his hands and knees coughing up more black blood.

"Well this must be my lucky day, a vampire and an albino to sell on the Black Market," the lady said with a menacing laugh as she walked out of the shadows. "And with my partner now gone I'll be twice as rich since I don't have to split the money anymore. Don't worry little one, the vampire will be dead soon enough since the arrows are silver and dipped in wolfsbane. He'd need a pretty powerful blood source to be able to survive that cocktail, which you can't provide with you being just a normal human."

Beau watched the woman go back to the table and pick up the hacksaw again. Beau glanced frantically between the woman and Tobias, who had completely collapsed onto the ground, his breath was coming in short, painful gasps.

Beau felt an odd tingling sensation flow down his arms to his fingertips and the symbols from the book began to fly in front of his eyes as he tried desperately to think of something that he could do to stop her. He wasn't too sure that he was ready to be able to use the spells that came with the symbols, but he knew that both him and Tobias were running out of time.

Beau chose the simple triangle spell and drew it with his fingertips in the air in front of him. Watching in amazement as the symbol sparkled in the air in front of him. Beau pushed the symbol in the direction of a stack of wooden devices that were at the far back left corner of the room.

"You shouldn't be able to do that," the woman commented as she backed away from Beau. The woman jumped forward onto the ground when all the wooden devices caught on fire all at the same time, and not just the ones in the corner that Beau had directed the spell towards, leaving an extremely narrow escape passage. The woman glared at Beau as she got up from the ground and quickly made her way over to the one area that was not on fire yet.

"I'm not done with you yet, kid!" the woman called back over her shoulder to Beau as she made her escape up the bloody stairs. "I'll come back and get you both!"

Chapter 33

Beau dropped his head back onto the ground, feeling very dizzy and like he was on the verge of throwing up. He just wanted to lay there and sleep forever. But a wheezing cough broke through his haze and he remembered that he was not alone down here.

Beau looked over to where Tobias lay, facing him, and saw that his normally demonic black and red eyes had clouded over to being just completely black. Tears dripped down from his eyes blending with the blood that was coming out of his nose, mouth, and the other open wounds on his body. He wasn't going to survive much longer if Beau didn't manage to do something to help him.

Beau slowly pushed himself off the ground and onto his hands and knees. His head was spinning, and his vision swam in front of his eyes. He reached around to the back of his head and gingerly touched the sore spot where his headache seemed to be originating from, sticky with dried blood. His stomach was tight and sore, and he vaguely remembered that he had been kicked several times in his stomach.

Beau managed to stagger to his feet, limping a couple steps before collapsing back onto the ground just in over Tobias's head with his hands landing on either side of Tobias's shoulders so that their heads didn't collide. Beau cried out, remembering that his one arm was broken but he just shifted the weight to the one good arm trying not to cause any more damage to his already broken arm.

Beau thought that Tobias looked completely different from the last time he had seen him. Tobias's eyes were sunken in with dark circles around them making his eyes appear bruised. His skin had gone so pale that in some areas it had actually started to turn blue. His eyes were closed and there was this painful sounding raspy noise that was coming from Tobias, which must've been his form of breathing by that point.

Tobias slowly opened his eyes as the scent of Beau's blood had drawn nearer to him. Beau felt relieved when he saw that some of the black had cleared from Tobias's eyes so that he could now see the red again, but it started to switch to panic when he noticed that Tobias's fangs were protruding out from his lips.

The increasing pulse was driving Tobias mad with hunger. He reached a wounded hand up to Beau and gripped the back of his neck, inching Beau's throat closer and closer to Tobias's throbbing fangs. Just as he was about to sink his teeth into the side of Beau's neck, he stopped feeling the agony in his throat and twisting around in his stomach again, he didn't have Beau's permission, so he couldn't feed from him.

Tobias loosened the grip that he had had on Beau's neck while making a pained noise and growling low in his throat. He could never ask Beau to do that for him, it was too much of him to ask and he knew that. Well this time when he died, he would die happy knowing that he had tried and more or less succeeded in saving his best friend.

"Tobias?" Beau asked confused as to why he didn't start feeding from him. Then he remembered what Tobias had told him about how he feeds. "Tobias, I give you my permission to feed from me."

Tobias's eyes shot back open and he used both of his hands to maneuver Beau's neck into a good position before sinking his teeth into the soft, warm flesh of Beau's neck. Beau gasped as he felt the sharp needle like teeth brake through his skin. It was probably the weirdest feeling that Beau had ever felt in his 12 years of life. As Tobias drank from Beau the pain that Beau had felt in the beginning was replaced by a more pleasurable feeling. As Beau's vision started to fade to black he knew that if he survived this, that he would never be able to say no to Tobias again.

Chapter 34

There was a bright light coming into Beau's line of sight, it felt warm and inviting, he started walking towards it. The darkness that was all around began to disappear the closer that he got until the bright light was all that he could see. As he opened his eyes the light began to take the shape of the lights in a hospital. As he looked around with his dizzy vision he could see some people sitting at the foot of his bed and some weird looking monitors off to his left side.

Only one of his arms felt light enough for him to be able to use, so he lifted it up and felt around himself to see how bad the damage was. There was a bandage around his head and around his throat, which would explain why it was painful to try to move his neck. He could see and feel the arm cast that went all the way up to his shoulder, and he could feel the cast that was covering his entire leg from his foot to his hip.

How had he ended up here? Beau couldn't remember anything except his own name and that he loved reading. *Did he get into a car accident or something? And who were those people that were sitting at the end of his bed? Did he know them?* Beau didn't seem to be drawn to either the young boy or the older woman.

The boy started to stir and opened his eyes to look towards Beau. His face completely lit up when he saw that Beau was awake. He jumped up from his chair and ran over to Beau's right side while Beau continued to stare at him with a confused expression.

"Do I know you?" Beau asked, his voice raspy from his dry throat, coughing after he spoke. The boy's face fell but he grabbed the water from the table that was next to him and held it out for Beau to sip from.

"I can't believe that she would be so caught up in her own mind that she would actually erase him from yours," the boy whispered quietly as he let Beau sip from the straw. The cool water immediately quenched Beau's parched throat. "My name is Kyle by the way, and we used to live together."

"We did? Do you know what happened then?" Beau asked looking at Kyle with hope filled eyes. Kyle opened his mouth but a rustling sound behind him made him snap his mouth shut.

"Well its good to see that you're doing better Beau, especially after that car accident that you were in," the woman said as she stretched before getting up from her seat and came to stand next to Kyle who had shrunk back from Beau and kept his head focused on the floor.

"Do I know you?" Beau asked as he squinted his eyes at the lady that was standing next to Kyle. He didn't like how the lady was making Kyle react and withdraw away from him.

"Why yes, you are one of my sons," the woman replied with a huge smile on her face, "and I'm your adoptive mother."

"Oh okay," Beau replied as he smiled back to the woman not too sure how he was supposed to react when being told this. Especially, since he got this bad feeling as he looked at her. There was something off about the woman who claimed she was his adoptive mother.

"Now come on Kyle, we better let him get some sleep, we'll come back and visit again some other time," the woman said as she gripped Kyle's shoulder and walked with him towards the door of Beau's hospital room. "See you later."

Then they both left, and Beau was left alone in a strange room with strange people all around him, in a world where he couldn't remember anything...

Epilogue

Beau was laying in the hospital bed at night not able to get a wink of sleep while his roommate was sound asleep behind the curtain. The drugs that the nurses had given him had made him woozy and dizzy but sadly not sleepy. Beau was achy and uncomfortable and couldn't seem to find a position that was comfortable enough to be able to sleep in. He tried one more time to close his eyes and try to get some sleep.

Beau heard the creaky sliding of a window opening, and vaguely heard soft footsteps on the linoleum floor coming towards him. Beau cracked an eye open to see who it was, but his vision was so blurred that all he could see was a child sized shadowy figure approach his bed on the right side.

Beau closed the eye that he had just opened and pretended to be asleep, hoping that whoever it was would just go away and let him sleep. He could feel cold fingers trace over the back of his hand making Beau sigh quietly. The person gripped his hand gently in their colder hand and bring it up to rest on what must've been their cheek. Beau felt an odd sense of longing towards the person, like his body still remembered him even if his brain no longer did.

"I promise that I will make them believe me, I won't let them ignore that you are my forever mate," the boyish voice said, he sounded desperate and on the verge of crying. "I'm sorry that I couldn't protect you like I promised, but I swear to you on my life that I won't let anything stop me from claiming you as mine. Please wait for me until then, my Răsărit[2]."

Beau felt his hand slowly be placed back onto the bed and the person lean over him. Beau felt something wet drop onto his cheek before a light brush of lips touched his forehead. The cool lips on his still slightly feverish forehead should've felt nice but all

---

[2] Răsărit means sunrise in Romanian

Beau could feel from the kiss was like the person was saying goodbye to him. Beau didn't want to lose this, the only thing that had felt familiar in this unfamiliar world where he knew nothing and no one.

"I promise that I won't let them get away with this," the boy whispered against Beau's forehead as the tears started to slip out of the corner of Beau's eyes. Then all the comfort left the moment that the person disappeared from his side, without a sound, and Beau was left alone in the hospital room feeling like he had just lost someone that was more important than any of his memories.

Silver and Fangs

Book 2 Excerpt

"I promise, I will get them to believe that you belong to me," the shadowy figure whispered his back turned to Beau as he began to walk away. Beau tried to chase after him, but the boy disappeared in the fog that had suddenly appeared, morphing the boy's shape into something bigger before he disappeared completely.

Beau sat straight up in bed and forced his eyes open, tears streaming down his cheeks and the vague sound of the alarm clock echoing in the background. Beau tried to calm his breathing as he quickly wiped the tears off his face before reaching over to turn off the alarm clock.

He sat there for a moment in silence and got his bearings. He was still in his small room in his apartment that he shared with Kyle that was within walking distance to the high school. Nothing that was around him was comforting him in the least, there was a longing ache in his chest as he stared out the window at the rising sun.

That same damned haunting dream that had bothered him for the last five years was back.

About the Author

CAITLYN FOURNIER is the author of the bestselling teenage romance book *Hated*, along with some popular poetry compilation books. She is also the author of a paranormal romance called *Hell's Heat*, and her first series book *Forgotten Magic* from the mutant series. She lives in Ontario, Canada with her two cats while also working long hours during the day. For more information go to, www.romancingtheparanormal.com.

Made in the USA
Lexington, KY
17 August 2019